SONG FOR A

Geoffrey Trease was born in ... up in Nottingham. In 1928 he won a scholarship to Queen's College, Oxford, but left the following year to work with children in London's East End slums. He later became a journalist. His first book, *Bows Against the Barons*, was published in 1934. Since then he has written over one hundred books, including forty adventure novels for young people, among them the Walker titles, *The Arpino Assignment*, *Shadow Under the Sea*, *Calabrian Quest* and *Bring Out the Banners*. He is also the author of adult novels, plays, biographies and other works of non-fiction – including the highly acclaimed critical study of children's fiction, *Tales Out of School*. Geoffrey Trease lives in Bath.

Also by Geoffrey Trease

The Arpino Assignment
Aunt Augusta's Elephant
Bows Against the Barons
Bring Out the Banners
Calabrian Quest
Cue for Treason
A Flight of Angels
The Iron Tsar
No Boats on Bannermere
The Red Towers of Granada
Shadow Under the Sea
Tomorrow Is a Stranger
The White Nights of St Petersburg

SONG FOR A TATTERED FLAG

GEOFFREY TREASE

WALKER BOOKS
AND SUBSIDIARIES
LONDON • BOSTON • SYDNEY

For Thomas

First published 1992 by Walker Books Ltd
87 Vauxhall Walk, London SE11 5HJ

This edition published 1993

2 4 6 8 10 9 7 5 3

©1992 Geoffrey Trease
Jacket illustration © 1992 Caroline Binch

The right of Geoffrey Trease to be
identified as author of this work
has been asserted by him in
accordance with the Copyright,
Designs and Patents act 1988.

Printed in Great Britain

British Library Cataloguing in Publication Data
A catalogue record for this book is
available from the British Library.

ISBN 0-7445-3082-2

AUTHOR'S NOTE

In closely following the historical facts of the Romanian rising of December 1989, the author is particularly indebted to two books, *Dispatches from the Barricades* by John Simpson of the BBC, and *The Life and Evil Times of Nicolae Ceausescu* by John Sweeney of the *Observer*.

CHAPTER ONE

The kids at school used to call me Dracula.

It bothered me once. I used to study my face anxiously in the glass. I only do that now to check if I need to shave. Often I don't. I have inherited my father's fair hair and fresh complexion, not my mother's raven-black and ivory — fine on someone from Romania but not so good on a boy who might, just might, turn out to be a vampire. At school my Romanian blood was unusual. The kids were not very hot on geography. They knew only one thing about Romania. It was where Dracula came from.

So, when I was small, I would go nervously to the mirror, open wide, and peer in as if I were a dentist. Any developments? Any fangs coming through? The joke died and so of course did my anxiety, but the nickname lingered until now, when I had just finished school. Luckily there was nothing foreign about my surname, Byrne.

Mother's feelings about her native land were mixed. She had homesick moods. She would sing me old Romanian songs when I was little, and alone together we talked quite a bit in Romanian, though my father did not encourage it. It was a sort of fairy-tale country she remembered, all forests and mountains and the swirling Danube. There were castles perched on crags, carved and painted churches in bright picture-book colours, lumbering ox-carts and barefoot children herding flocks of geese. Every cottage had its well, with a tiny roof over it and a bucket dangling, and outside the garden hedges the rows of irises stretched on and on to the end of the village.

"And the gipsy fiddlers! You'd have loved them, Greg."

And I would, too. I had taken up the violin at school. I had won a place in the youth orchestra formed from our whole area.

"Perhaps we could go to Romania some day?" I suggested.

But her face changed. "No! I can never go back – never in this world!"

It was only as I grew up that I pieced clues together and guessed that her other memories were much less happy. She never had letters from Romania. I knew that both her parents had died when she was young and she had been brought up by an uncle, also now long dead. She said that she had lost touch with all her relatives.

Then one day a letter did come. Two actually, one enclosed inside another with a Glasgow post-mark. Mother gave a little exclamation of surprise as she ran her eye over the first.

"How nice of them! From complete strangers! This lady and her husband, they were on holiday in Bucharest – they got friendly with a girl who served them in a gift-shop – she asked them to post this for her when they got home – " She passed this first letter across the breakfast-table to my father and eagerly tore open the shoddy-looking envelope which had been inside. She drew out a thin single sheet in purple handwriting, read it silently with knitted brows, then handed it on to my father. "A relative!" she said in a surprised tone. "But it is in English," she added reassuringly. "Does the girl think I have forgotten my own language? No, it was caution, I expect."

In due course the letter came round to me. The style had a rather formal, continental flavour.

Dear Mrs Byrne, I believe we are distant cousins, but as I am younger I should greet you with respect. You will not mind my writing to you? It is so interesting to have a relative in the West. I wish that we could meet. We found your address among my mother's papers when she died last year. She had kept the letter you sent her many years ago. My sister Ana said we must destroy it. Her husband is so nervous of the Securitate.

That, I knew, was the secret police, who discouraged all unofficial contacts with the West.

I pretended to drop it into the stove (the

9

letter went on), but I hid it, and now I take this chance to write to you. We used to speak of you carefully among ourselves. I would like to ask so many questions, but if I gave you an address to reply to I should soon have the Securitate knocking on my door. Perhaps one day I shall achieve my dream to travel, as you did, and we shall be able to meet. I too love very much to swim, but I shall never win prizes like you. I work in this small shop in Bucharest. I will sign myself only, with respect, your distant (in both meanings) cousin, Nadia. I will not take the risk to write my surname.

"Socol," said my mother, "as mine was."

"Good English," said my father approvingly. "Useful in her job, obviously." He referred back to the Glasgow lady's covering letter. "A little gift-shop near the famous Stavropoleos church—"

"I remember that church." My mother took up both letters. "I must write and thank *her*. Too bad I can't answer this Nadia. She must have been born after I left." She stuffed both the letters into her desk. I do not recall any further mention of them. There was so much more to think about.

It was my final year at school. My future was not settled – *I* was not settled – and Dad was not going to rush me. Had I really a vocation for music, had I real talent? Should I go for something quite different? The university or – what? Dad recommended getting myself sorted out before making a final decision.

That was when our conductor, Dr Mannheim, sprang his ambitious plan for the youth orchestra to make its first concert tour abroad.

Playing in our regional orchestra does not confer all that much prestige. But Mannheim is a first-rate conductor, really inspiring and tremendously ambitious for us. When he told me that he wanted me, if my parents agreed, at my usual desk among the second violins, I rushed home in high excitement.

"Where?" asked my father.

"Start at Salzburg – Czechoslovakia, perhaps not Prague but Bratislava anyhow, then into Hungary to Budapest – I can't remember all the places, some of the bookings aren't finalized –"

My mother's eyes were dancing. "It will be an education for him! How long is this tour?"

"Mannheim says we should be home comfortably for Christmas –"

'I should hope so," Dad said. "Have you forgotten our little idea of winter sports this Christmas?"

To be honest I had – it had seemed so far away when we discussed it and this new possibility had driven it clean out of my mind.

"We can't do that any later," he said. "I shall be too tied up at the office from New Year onwards."

"It'll be all right," I cried out in relief. "Our last concert is in the second week of December. Bucharest."

"*No!*" The enthusiasm died out of my mother's voice. She looked across at my father. "He should not go to Bucharest."

"Oh, come, dear – it's not you going to Bucharest, it's Greg."

They used to argue about the news from Eastern Europe. It was the summer of 1989, when the Soviets were still the great bogy of the western democracies. Their smaller neighbours were all under their thumb – it was not until several months later that democracy began bursting out all over the place. Dad was inclined to think that Romania was a shade better than the other puppet states. She took more of an independent line and, even though she was Communist, did not let Russia push her around.

So Dad tried to overcome Mum's fears of Bucharest.

"Greg would be OK. With his British passport. And this top man there – this – this –" He hesitated as he always did over the awkward name of the Romanian dictator.

"Ceausescu?" she suggested scornfully.

"That's the one. He's really keen to keep friends with the West—"

"For his own purposes. To play you off against the Russians!"

"But you must admit, he's the only one of these people who pays his foreign debts—"

"By squeezing the money out of his citizens! Their standard of life goes down and down."

"Well, I've not so much against him, except for his unpronounceable name."

"He is not unpronounceable," Mum retorted. "Just unspeakable." Once again, very patiently, she drilled my father syllable by syllable in the Romanian name until at last he could come up with a passable rendering.

"Chow-shess-koo? OK? After all, the American President has had him to the White House – "

"He has to entertain some very odd guests."

"And he's stayed at Buckingham Palace too!"

My mother sniffed. "The poor Queen! She wears a crown, but she must do what her prime minister says."

In the end, though reluctant, Mum agreed to my going on the trip. "But promise me," she said earnestly, "if you go into Romania you will do nothing silly? You will play, you will rehearse, you will do only what the other boys and girls do?"

I laughed. "Mannheim will see to that."

"It will be safest not to speak a single word of Romanian. Not to reveal that you are different from any other British boy."

I was allowed one solitary variation, which had really nothing to do with Romania. If our tour finished with the Bucharest concert in mid-December I should no sooner be home before we were all starting out for our winter sports Christmas in the Tyrol. It would be much more sensible, if Mannheim agreed, to leave the rest of the orchestra to go back to England without me, and make my way independently to meet my parents at the skiing centre in Austria.

"But won't you get there several days too soon?" my mother objected.

"I could take my time." I began to wax enthusiastic about the wonderful complexity of the European railway system and the way I could break my journey at various places. My interest in railways was rather a joke in the family, and Mum was a great believer in travel (except perhaps in Romania!) as a way to broaden the mind. I think she liked my idea of a leisurely cross-country meander through Yugoslavia and Hungary and Austria.

I purposely left my plans flexible and did not worry her with any talk of Romania. But a week before the trip I went to her desk. I knew which drawers were not private and I was always welcome to open. I borrowed those letters from Nadia and the Glasgow lady, got them photocopied, and put them back. I'd tell Mum afterwards if anything interesting came of it, but I could not imagine that anything would.

And was I wrong!

CHAPTER
TWO

Bucharest was the end. The whole orchestra agreed on that. And we did not mean just the end of our tour. Bucharest was the last word. Dim, drab and depressing. It had once been legendary as "the Paris of the Balkans". Its symbol now should have been the 40-watt bulb.

Austria at the start had spoilt us. But Czechoslovakia and Hungary, though Communist for over forty years, were fast shaking off the Soviet grip. Freedom was in the air, people had a new light in their eyes. Czechoslovakia was about to boil over and we were lucky not to have our concert cancelled there because of the political excitement. Hungary was just quietly edging itself out of the Communist world. You could buy the British newspapers. No wild street demonstrations, but a quiet assumption that the Russians would not come driving in with their tank columns as they had in 1956.

"The Iron Curtain is getting threadbare," said Dr Mannheim.

Not in Romania, though. We sensed that even before we got through Customs. The faces were sour, unwelcoming. Other frontier checks had been little more than a formality. We were an organized group, most of us only in our teens, unlikely to be spies or terrorists. But these officials went through every bag with a tooth-comb. They scowled at a drum or a cello as if it were merely an ideal hiding-place for heroin or plastic explosive.

Mannheim was fit to be tied. He marched round, protesting furiously in German, which they seemed to understand. In the end he got all our instruments safely through without apparent damage, but they took their revenge by confiscating a bottle of Scotch from his personal baggage. That did not improve his temper either.

What were they searching for? What were they not? Anything that was banned – and that added up to a long list. Almost anything printed, from a foreign newspaper to a girlie magazine.

My friend Joe was particularly outraged. He is American but lives in England. He, too, plays second violin. When we lodged two to a room I usually shared with him. We call him "Holy Joe". He is not noticeably pious though we all feel he should be, his uncle in New York being a Methodist bishop, no less.

"That slob over there has taken my Bible!" he howled indignantly.

I had seen it laid out on his bedside table but I had never seen him reading it. I knew it was special. He had promised his grandmother that he would keep it all his life.

I tried to pacify him. "They're dead against religion—"

"But they accepted thousands — as a gift — just a few years back! My uncle told me. The American churches combined — and they said they were very grateful. So why should these guys take mine off me? I don't get it —"

The puzzle was partly solved that evening.

I was standing in the washroom. We were accommodated in a university hostel — no luxury hotels for the youth orchestra. Joe burst out of a cubicle behind me, madder even than he'd been at the airport.

"Will you look at this?" He waved a sheet of lavatory paper.

It was shoddy grey stuff, recycled, but so poorly that some faint traces of print still showed. "Everything here seems of lousy quality," I said.

"Hold it up to the light! See the word, 'Moses'? And 'Abraham'?"

I could also make out a few Romanian words which I translated for him. Something about "the Lord God".

Joe carefully tore off half a dozen examples to show to his uncle. Later I heard the end of the story. That paper must have come from the twenty thousand bibles that the World Reformed Alliance churches had sent to Romania. The scandal had indeed already been detected by a professor at Yale. Ceausescu had received the books politely so as not to offend the American Government, but less than two hundred copies had reached the congregations they were meant for. The rest had been contemptuously recycled.

Next morning Mannheim called a rehearsal. It was held in the Romanian Athenaeum, an ornate domed building with a roof-decoration of Greek lyres. We were to perform there tomorrow, an honour (Mannheim hinted) due less to our musical merit than to the propaganda value of the occasion.

Mannheim is a perfectionist but also an enthusiast. His wit is famous, his sarcasm murderous, but it is never directed at us. He remembers that we are young and that sarcasm can be the most hurtful, blighting weapon imaginable. What he wants is to get the best out of each player and show him how to produce it. He is not so old himself, but to us he seems immensely wise and experienced.

It was a long rehearsal. We knew the music backwards by now, but he had to draw us gently together again after the move from Budapest. And every hall is different. Even he, who had been in so many cities, had never set foot in Bucharest. He had to study the acoustics, explain any peculiarities we must allow for and just why he was asking for some tiny variation in our playing.

After lunch Joe and I joined the sightseeing coach-drive round the city. We liked to explore on our own, but we had found in other cities that such a trip was the best way to get one's bearings.

Bucharest was not much like the city my mother

had described. Of course it was mid-December. The chain of lakes was hung with low silvery fog, with no sign of those bronzed swimmers that figured so vividly in her recollection. She had spoken of picturesque wooden houses with vines trailing over carved balconies, in narrow byways shaded with limes and chestnuts. Now it seemed more a place of high apartment-blocks, grim concrete geometry. Maybe, exploring on foot, I could still find those byways that no coach could penetrate.

Our young guide, Marietta, harangued us vibrantly with names and statistics. We drew up by a triumphal arch, built only three years before. Her tone became reverent as she translated the inscription. "The Golden Epoch – the Epoch of Nicolae Ceausescu."

Joe muttered, "You're telling *me*!"

We drove on, pausing in front of massive public buildings, with just time to jump out and click a camera. Bucharest seemed full of museums. There was a museum for everything, from Music and Railways, both of which I would have liked to visit, to the History of the Communist Party, which sounded like one big yawn. Marietta quacked on. The one thing she did not explain was why, outside every big store, so many glum-looking people were standing in line, clutching empty shopping-bags apparently made of oilcloth. One girl tried to ask a question, but Marietta did not encourage questions. She had learned her piece and preferred to unwind it like a living tape recorder.

What was not a museum was usually an old church or a new sports complex. "I wish much you could see this park in summer," she would say, pointing across a wasteland of frost-bitten grass. "So much dancing! So much music! Everyone gay!" She looked perplexed by our ribald response. She had clearly learnt her English from an old-fashioned instructor.

We pulled up at the entrance to a side-street. The name, Strada Stavropoleos, sounded a bell in my memory. "And here we have another historic church," said Marietta. A suppressed groan ran back through the coach. "You will wish photographs."

I followed Joe and the other enthusiasts. I had no camera but I had an idea. I bent and murmured to Mannheim, "Do you mind, sir, if I make my own way back? I feel a little sick – "

You cannot fool Mannheim. His eyes gleamed with understanding – and envy. "So do I, Gregory. But I am in charge of the party so I can hardly follow your example."

"Thank you, sir – "

"Take care. I want you in your place at rehearsal tomorrow."

It *was* quite a picturesque church, with a columned portico, some whirligig arabesques, and a little tower sitting on the top like a hat. Joe was taking a picture. "I'm dropping out," I murmured. "See you back at the hostel." I was gone before he could offer to join me. For this I needed to be on my own. I slipped round a corner until the coach had moved on.

Then, sure enough, I saw the shop across the street. It looked like the one the Glasgow lady had described. A bent old woman stood in the doorway, leaning on an ebony stick, scowling after the coach and muttering Romanian words which I felt sure my mother had never taught me.

I had planned to stroll past casually, pausing to glance at the goods while actually taking a peep inside for any sign of a girl who might be my unknown cousin. But the woman fixed me with eyes that were bright and black under their wrinkled hoods. Her unkempt grey hair had yellow streaks of fading dye. She clearly decided that even one customer was better than none. She called out a wheedling invitation in German. I must not betray that I had even a smattering of that language. It was Nadia who must serve me if she was still there. I crossed over, put on a dumb expression. "Do you speak English?"

She shook her head. Then she turned and uttered a screech that must have penetrated to the remotest recesses of the shop. "*Naaa – dya!*" My heart leapt.

With her arm outstretched, Madame steered me inside. She did not mean me to escape. She did not know how little I wanted to. Especially when I saw Nadia, even in that gloomy interior. I have never forgotten that first impression.

I thought instinctively of a young lion. It was her soft silent step, the smooth mane of tawny hair framing her face, the lights in her green eyes. Mane is wrong, I suppose – lionesses do not have manes. Nadia was quite unambiguously female.

21

She carried a small cup of black Turkish coffee which she set down beside the cash desk. The old woman limped over eagerly. She muttered something about "British — or American". The girl smiled at me and came across.

"Can I help you?"

"I want to find something — for my mother." And I've found it, I thought triumphantly, though I must pretend I have not. Nadia's letter to Mum had indicated how dangerous it might be if the security police knew she had any link with the West. I prowled round the shop. The stock was an odd mixture of tourist souvenirs and good-quality second-hand items that must once have been treasured in prosperous homes before the present regime came into power. I moved away, as far as I could, from Madame's gimlet gaze.

I had prepared for this problem of unwanted witnesses. "I made a list," I murmured. But what I pulled out was the photocopy of Nadia's own letter. Her eyes widened in alarm at the sign of it. She flushed. She must have realized in that moment that there was no danger, I was so obviously nothing to do with the Securitate, but an ordinary British tourist. She kept her cool.

"We have peasant embroidery." She held up samples for my inspection. I made appreciative noises. Intertwined with this make-believe dialogue we managed somehow to carry on another conversation without varying our tone.

"What price had you in mind? Who *are* you?"

"It was my mother you wrote to. I'm Greg Byrne."

"So we are cousins!" She covered up this burst of animation by waxing enthusiastic about the blouse she was holding against herself.

"Yes." I pretended to study the garment. "Of course," I said gravely – Madame, over in her corner, could not see the mischief in my eye – "my mother's measurements would be rather different – "

My cousin smothered a giggle. Madame did not miss that. She croaked a curt instruction. Nadia answered meekly and began to show me tablecloths.

"It is difficult," she murmured, running her finger over the exquisite coloured stitchery. "We cannot easily talk here. How long do you stay in Bucharest?"

"I'm with the British youth orchestra – "

"So!" She looked impressed.

"It's our last concert tomorrow. Then – "

Her face fell. "So soon?"

My mind was racing. I had already toyed with the idea that I need not take the first train out of Bucharest just because the orchestra was leaving. If anything turned up that made me want to stay on another day or two...

I got no chance to tell her this. Madame lost patience. She set down her empty coffee-cup and came creaking over to us. I had played my hand badly. By this time I ought to have pulled out my wallet and bought something, anything, however

23

useless. I had been too slow. Nadia had not yet made a sale. Madame told her, in a vicious undertone, that she was a dead loss. She was there to earn her keep, not gossip with young foreigners. She herself, though she spoke no English, could do better. Nadia was dispatched in disgrace to the kitchen.

Madame then got to work on me. She clutched my arm and, with her other hand, pointed at her varied stock, stroking the material, fingering the carved woodwork, pouring out incomprehensible details in different languages. Prices she indicated on outspread fingers or in pencilled scribbles on a grubby envelope.

She wore me down. She would have worn anybody down. Seeing no hope of Nadia's reappearance I bought a scarf which I thought might do for my mother and a painted toy which might please some not-very-bright child. Realizing that she would sell me nothing more, Madame then firmly saw me on my way with what sounded like a stream of thanks and blessings, though I felt far from sure.

I trudged away down the narrow street like a defeated army. I was angry with myself. I felt I had been feeble, but I had been so scared of making trouble for the girl. I had found her – that was something – but I had not managed to get her home address or tell her where I was staying.

I must visit the shop again. So long as I bought something Madame could hardly complain. I would use the shopping-list trick again, only this time I would have scribbled a note I could slip into Nadia's hand.

Somehow, I was determined, we'd work out a way to meet.

CHAPTER
THREE

I could not attempt anything the next day.

The morning was filled with a long rehearsal. "We must wind up this first overseas tour with a faultless performance," Mannheim declared. "You may be getting a little tired by now, looking forward to home and Christmas. But you must hang on for one more evening. Afterwards, you can relax. Tonight, though, not the slightest raggedness, not the least hint of fatigue. You must sparkle like the stars."

When the other sections were dismissed for lunch we strings were kept behind for one more run-through of Elgar's *Introduction and Allegro*. It gave all the other instrumentalists a useful breather, and the whole orchestra would come together again at full strength for a tremendous climax to the concert. But we had to get that Elgar just right.

After lunch I went off and found myself an

inexpensive little hotel I could move to for a day or two when the orchestra left tomorrow and I was on my own. No point in going back to Nadia's shop until these matters were arranged.

By then it was rather late to go rushing off to Strada Stavropoleos, and there was no urgent need.

Keen though I was to meet my cousin again, I did not much fancy a second encounter with her formidable employer. I must make no mistake this time. I must be at my best, braced for the occasion. Tomorrow would be much better, when I had nothing else on my mind. Today, in fairness to Mannheim, I must think of nothing but the concert. He had already told us not to wear ourselves out tearing round the city but rest, and tonight be literally at concert pitch.

It was to be quite an occasion. It would be an honour anyhow for us to perform in this hall that was the home of Romania's Philharmonic Orchestra. The President would be there and our own ambassador. The building was festooned with flags, the Union Jack alternating with the blue, yellow and red tricolour of our hosts. We struck up their national anthem as the presidential party entered, and followed it with "God Save the Queen".

It was a packed house. The Romanians genuinely love music, and though ours was a young orchestra we were bringing them a flavour of the West. They were many of them young themselves, warm and responsive. Out of that sea of rapt faces one leapt to my eye during a brief passage when my section fell silent and I lowered my violin for a moment's rest.

Nadia!

She had slipped into a cheap side seat, too close to get the most balanced sound effect, so near that I knew it was her. That pale mane gleamed out amid the dark-jacketed shoulders of the men around her.

Was she with them, or with one of them? Or had she managed to get hold of a ticket after meeting me yesterday? But a musician's thoughts must not wander. Automatically my fiddle tucked itself under my chin again, my right elbow went up, Mannheim's magnetic eye was upon us, and all together at precisely the right moment we plunged back into the racing tide of the music.

Only in the interval dared I think of Nadia again. Only when we filed back on to the platform could I let my eyes rove briefly, note that she was apparently alone. With luck, if I slipped quickly out of the artists' room when we finished, I might catch her at the exit. With a crowd this size the hall would take time to empty.

The second half went well. The Elgar, though unfamiliar, was warmly applauded. We wound up with Dvorak's symphony, *From the New World*. I thought they would never let us go.

They did at last, Mannheim with an enormous bunch of flowers, Julia our leader with one as big. We trooped off after them, our ears positively ringing.

Backstage I slipped my fiddle into its case, ready for a lightning departure. I was out of luck.

"Stand fast, everybody," Mannheim ordered. "We are to be greatly honoured." A buzz ran round the artists' room. The President and his wife coming round to congratulate us. An honour indeed. I could have done without it, just then.

Some unsmiling men with questing eyes came in first. They were not especially big – the President himself was not tall and he did not like to be dwarfed by those around him – but they were solid and really formidable, strong-arm men, the President's personal bodyguard. I doubted if they were really music lovers. They might have been poured into their suits like liquid concrete. We lined up respectfully.

The notables entered. Mannheim bowed stiffly as our ambassador presented him. Ceausescu looked seventy-ish with a shock of ash-grey hair and the coldest blue eyes imaginable. They made his strong-arm men look like sentimental spaniels. An obsequious interpreter was murmuring in his ear. When he spoke he had a slight stammer. Not an impressive figure, you might think. But those eyes, so devoid of human warmth, set you wondering.

Madame Ceausescu was heavily built, rather ungainly, with a big nose and dark eyes set in a pinched face. She was coarse-featured, thickly made up and dressed to kill. Some Romanian later quoted to me their malicious proverb, "you don't put a saddle on a cow".

Mannheim presented Julia. "This, Mr. President, is the leader of the orchestra."

That was when Julia committed her appalling gaffe. She thrust out her hand. There was a horrified drawing-in of breath from the entourage. The President himself seemed to shrink. But Julia, determined to be friendly, clamped his hand in hers and shook it. From his expression her fingers might have been red hot.

Later she was quite unrepentant. "Where I come from," she said, "we were taught it's the lady who puts out her hand to the gentleman."

"Not with heads of state," said Joe.

"I haven't met that many."

I saw the sequel to this incident just afterwards. Mannheim and the ambassador ushered the presidential party into a little side room where they were offered drinks. Through the open door I saw Ceausescu irritably motioning the waiter away. He was, I know now, terrified of being poisoned. He annoyed the Queen when, even at Buckingham Palace, he took his taster to try everything before he touched it. Even poor Julia's handshake was possibly dangerous.

So I watched, fascinated, a fantastic ritual performed. A bodyguard whipped out a little bottle. Its contents looked like water or gin, but they must have been surgical spirit. The President held out his hands, the man poured the antiseptic over them. Ceausescu turned his hands over for the repeat procedure. Another bodyguard offered a sealed envelope which he tore open. He pulled out a paper towel, dried his fingers on it carefully and dropped it to the floor. The man stooped and picked it up. It was clearly a recognized drill.

I never forgot that episode. I had seen a powerful but very frightened man, who lived in the shadow of death.

Some of the strong-arm men stayed by the door of the artists' room. Apart from etiquette there was no chance for anyone to leave before the President. I groaned inwardly. The hall would long ago have emptied, Nadia must be halfway home. If any of us harboured murderous thoughts against Ceausescu I was that one.

At last he went, his retinue following. I pulled on my top coat, seized my violin-case, and still hoping against hope rushed out through the artists' exit.

Straight into the arms of a girl.

Not, alas, Nadia. "Autograph!" she screeched in my ear. "Please — autograph!"

"I'm nobody —"

But she thrust a pen into my hand, an open notebook under my nose. I signed in the semi-darkness. The city's street-lighting was a bad joke. Notebook and pen were snatched back, a smacking kiss imprinted on my gaping mouth. The voice cried in shrill triumph. "And also I have kissed British boy!" She turned to assail some more of the orchestra as they came streaming out.

Quite a throng of fans had been waiting patiently in the dank night air. At any other time I would have found it exciting, but just then I cared only about missing Nadia. Still, one could not be rude. Luckily most of the pack wanted our conductor. I scribbled some more autographs, managed not to drop my violin-case amid the rapturous huggings, and escaped round the corner to our waiting coach. I had my foot on the step when a plaintive voice behind me panted, "Please! *I* do not want an autograph –"

I turned fast enough then. Nadia was smiling up at me out of a dark headscarf that hid her hair.

CHAPTER FOUR

Joe was waiting to get in behind me. I pushed my violin-case into his free hand. "Take this back for me – won't be long." He asked no questions. He's a good guy.

Nadia drew me away from the flurry and chatter round the coach. "Is there anywhere we could go," I asked, "for a cup of coffee?" I looked pessimistically round the great square, now fast emptying. It was largely surrounded by blank-looking official buildings, their windows dark. Over to the right was an impressive, if old-fashioned, de luxe hotel, with light streaming through its revolving doors and people sweeping in and out.

"The Athénée Palace is not for us," said my cousin decisively. "It costs the earth. Also, the staff all work for the Securitate. There is not much night-life for ordinary people. I know a café."

We turned the other way, struck across the corner of the square and started down the main street, the Calea Victoriei. It runs through the city like a spine – only, like so much in Bucharest, it is slightly crooked.

"I had to see you again," she said.

"Me too! The old lady rather interrupted us."

"Old *lady*!" She spat out the words. "When you said you were leaving tomorrow I was almost frantic."

"The orchestra is leaving. I am not."

"You are not?" Her fingers tightened on my sleeve. We stopped for a moment. Her voice was incredulous. And delighted.

I explained. I should be at the Hotel Carpathia for several days before setting out to join my parents in Austria. "I was determined to see you again," I assured her. "I was going to the shop tomorrow. Then tonight I saw you –"

"You recognized me!" She was pleased.

"You bet. I meant to dash round and catch you as you left. But that wretched Ceausescu –"

Again her grip tightened on my arm. She whispered, "It is better you do not speak that name. The Securitate are everywhere. Hotel rooms are – what is word? – bugged. The hostels, too. Students are considered dangerous. Waiters, taxi-drivers, doorkeepers – they all pass on anything they hear. It is safer not to mention certain names. We say simply 'the Comrade', or just 'he' – or 'she'. We know who we mean."

Before we entered the café she warned me to

34

keep my voice down and not to speak English. It would attract attention. People might gather round our table — it would be friendly and harmless, but there might always be someone . . . She had gathered by now that I spoke a little Romanian, though it did not compare with her own grasp of English.

There were candles on the tables, not so much to lend romantic atmosphere as to guard against the frequent power cuts. There were many young people, some obviously from the concert. We found a table to ourselves in a corner.

She apologized for the poor coffee. "After what you are used to – "

"It's fine," I lied.

It was hot anyhow, and welcome after the performance. "*Mascota?*" She pointed to a chocolate cake. "*Gogosi?*" This was a sort of doughnut. I am always hungry after a concert when the tension is suddenly over, but I would have eaten anyhow, for Nadia's sake. The poor girl was ravenous. I had never seen anyone so sylph-like put the food away as she did, as though there were no tomorrow.

We talked in whispers as any couple might. My long-forgotten Romanian was coming back. After two days of hearing it all around me, my eyes constantly scanning signs and posters, my vocabulary was growing. It was easy to exchange basic information. Nadia would be spending Christmas with her married sister, Ana, who lived in the western city of Timisoara. I told her about my mother, and my British father, and how they had met in England. A real contact of thought and feeling was not easy. I felt frustrated, remembering her own fluency in English when she was free to display it.

She sensed my exasperation. She murmured, "Tomorrow the shop closes at two."

"You'll be free?"

She nodded. "Yes. I could show you the lakes at Herastrau. Not so many people like to walk there in December."

"I should!"

"I also, I think."

Out in the open no one would notice our talking English.

"I'll be waiting outside the shop," I promised.

"Madame would see you. Go into the church." She frowned at her watch. "I must go now. You can find your way to the hostel? The university is quite near."

"Have *you* far to go?"

She hesitated. "Not too far."

"Then I'll walk you home – "

"And then you *will* get lost!" She laughed. "It is like a rabbit-warren where I live. No, I will take a taxi. But you are very kind."

And she was very firm. I could have argued that if I kept the cab I should not get lost, but I had the notion that it was sometimes better to follow her lead without argument.

Turning back into the Calea Victoriei we saw a man just paying off his driver. "This is lucky," said Nadia, putting up her hand. Fuel was too short for cabs to cruise round in quest of a fare. This one, like the buses and some cars, carried a tank of methane gas on the roof.

Nadia had meant lucky in another sense, though. "My favourite driver," she explained under her breath as we hurried along the kerb. "Adrian Donea. He is so interesting. He is a designer – he has had to take to taxi-driving because the money is so much better."

She introduced us as he opened the door for her. He was good-looking in a rather Italian way – the Romanians claim that they are descended from the ancient Romans, they are not Slavs. She must know him well and trust him, I thought, for she made no secret of my identity, and I had a feeling she would tell him more about me as they drove. "Good night, Greg!" She leant out and kissed me, and they drove off. I looked after them thoughtfully. I could have wished – quite illogically – that Adrian Donea was not *quite* so handsome, but what had that to do with me? I ought to be thankful that, in this dour and faintly menacing city, I had been able to hand her over to a cab-driver she clearly knew and trusted.

I turned into the Boulevard Republicii which led straight past the university. In the hostel I found an end-of-term atmosphere. People were racing along corridors, in and out of each other's rooms, exchanging phone numbers, making dates throughout the holiday season. Staying behind in Bucharest could have been utterly depressing. Having found Nadia made all the difference.

Next morning I waved them all off to the airport, then took my stuff round to the Carpathia. I felt a little odd without my faithful fiddle, but I knew that Mannheim would get everything and everybody safely home. Except me. I suddenly felt wonderfully free.

Once I had filled in the forms at the hotel I went out into the sunshine and, after wandering round for a while, headed for the big underground coffee-bar in University Square. It was clearly popular with students, and a foreigner was not conspicuous.

Afterwards I thought I would like to buy some little present for my cousin. There was a twenty-storey hotel, the Inter-Continental, standing just back from the boulevard, and I guessed that like all the leading hotels it would have a Comturist shop where western luxuries, unobtainable by most Romanians, could be bought for hard currency. Once confronted with the dazzling display of goods I realized how little I knew of Nadia's tastes. We both seemed to be non-smokers. Mum had taught me that if you gave scent to a girl you ought to know her preferences. There were some high-grade foreign tights and things like that, which I guessed almost any Romanian girl would have accepted with rapture – but I did not know Nadia's size.

In the end I played for safety. I bought a box of chocolates, as I might have done for a girl at home. And also, because this was decidedly not home, but a land of unbelievable shortages, I bought a little carton of real Brazilian coffee beans. I felt sure she would not be offended by such a homely gift. Without dollars or sterling they'd have remained as inaccessible to her as if they'd stayed in Brazil.

I reached the Stavropoleos church ahead of time. It was really picturesque, built around 1730, when this region was still under the Turks. The interior was plainish, so I came out again into the daylight to study the delicate carvings and arabesques. Soon I heard the clatter of wooden shutters across the street and saw Nadia closing the shop. I stepped back into the shadow of the portico. After a few minutes she emerged in her outdoor clothes. She saw me as she drew near, laid a finger on her lips, and sailed by without slackening pace. I waited before sauntering casually after her, and overtook her round the corner in another narrow street, the Lipscani, a colourful thoroughfare of small cafés and antique shops and street-vendors who observed no closing times.

"So sorry to be late," she said. "Madame kept me."

"Think nothing of it."

"For this afternoon I shall forget her." She frowned. I thought, she has something on her mind.

I would have liked to take her arm, but in that bustling crowd I often had to follow at her heels as she threaded her way. "We take a trolley-bus," she said over her shoulder.

"Anything you say."

We reached the wide boulevard and bought tickets from a kiosk. The fare was insignificant, but she introduced me conscientiously to the mysteries of the small change. The *lei* (about sixteen to the pound) came in notes as well as coins. One *leu* equalled a hundred *bani* but a five-*bani* piece was nowadays almost worthless.

The trolley-bus pulled up, crowded. We shoved our way aboard. "We punch the tickets ourselves," she said. We had to stand, tightly wedged, holding on to each other when the vehicle stopped or went forward again.

Ceausescu's vainglorious Arc de Triomph rose before us. On this clearer day I caught my first glimpse of the distant mountains, a long snow-dappled skyline to the north. Yes, I thought, there *was* great beauty in my mother's country.

We got out and struck across the vast open park towards a belt of trees, leafless now, a delicate filigree against the blueness of water under a cloudless sky.

"There are a dozen lakes," she said, "like a necklace round this side of the city."

Now we could talk freely and in English. There were only a few figures in sight on this winter afternoon. An old, old man, pausing every few yards to lean on his stick and regain his breath, and a pair of lovers – but *they* were a thousand miles away.

"Tell me about your mother," said Nadia. "I have never been quite clear about what happened."

"You've heard about her swimming? How really good she was?"

"Of course! It's a legend in the family – only

we could never boast as proudly as we'd have liked to do. She'd become — what is the English phrase? — a skeleton in our cupboard. A defector. At seventeen! Younger than I am now."

"It was the swimming that took her to Britain in the team for some festival. Both her parents had died before she was six, and she was brought up by her aunt and uncle, finally by her uncle alone. A wonderful man, she always says. Her mother's brother — which was fortunate as it turned out."

"How?"

"The surname was different, so the Securitate did not spot the connection."

"I am getting lost — "

"I don't wonder! Another skeleton in the cupboard. Little girls wouldn't be told!"

"Tell me now!"

"OK. While Mum was on this tour she picked up a British newspaper and read that her uncle had been arrested for political activity." I heard Nadia draw in her breath sharply. "None of the other swimmers noticed it — and the organizers, their minders, were no wiser."

"The different surname!"

"That's right. Mum must have gone through Hell for a couple of days. Daren't tell anyone, daren't ask anybody — "

"Poor kid!" Nadia was really moved.

"She watched the papers. Luckily her uncle was known abroad — he was quite news-worthy. The next thing she read was 'shot while escaping'."

"She must have been *shattered*. What did she do?"

"She *was* shattered, but she thought quickly – she had to. She remembered her uncle's last words when he saw her off. He'd spoken with a strange sort of emphasis. 'Don't worry about me,' he'd said, 'enjoy yourself – and don't hurry back.'"

"He could see what was coming."

"She thinks so. She took it almost as an instruction. She knew that at any moment the team-manager might get *his* instructions, if the Securitate got wise to her family connection. She could have been watched night and day till she was bundled safely on a plane back to Bucharest."

"So?"

"She slept on it. Or rather she didn't sleep much – she says she thought and wept and went on thinking. In the morning she walked out of the hotel, went to the police – and claimed political asylum."

"And got it?" Nadia's eyes were wide with admiration.

"Sure. She was news for a week, her face in the papers and on TV. I expect her face helped." I was proud of Mum and could not hide the fact. "And the events she'd won as a swimmer."

"She has been happy in the West?"

"I guess so. I suppose, to some extent, she'll always be a divided person. Sometimes I feel divided myself." The words slipped out. I had never voiced that thought to anyone.

"You too?"

"I'm British, born and bred – but in blood I'm half Romanian; somewhere I must have another set of relations, just as real. I sometimes wonder, just where do I actually belong?"

Nadia sighed. "It was difficult – dangerous even – to maintain contact."

"We've made up for it now."

We walked on. I wanted to know about her. She had come to Bucharest with an office job in one of the big state institutions. The work had not been bad but the regimentation was irksome. She disliked the compulsory attendance at meetings and political rallies. Most of all, though, she hated the monthly interrogation and inspection.

At first I did not catch on.

She explained. "This horrible woman. She came round every department, checking up on our most private affairs. Are you pregnant? Have you been obtaining contraceptives? You realize that this would be a serious offence? It would also be a miracle – " Nadia laughed bitterly. "No one can get such things in our country."

"But anyhow – " I hesitated. Did this sound absurdly innocent? How much did I know about my cousin? "You're not married."

"I tell her so. She says, 'What does that matter? You are a healthy girl! It is the patriotic duty of every woman to have at least five children for the good of Romania.' And I say, this law is for married women, I will never have babies before I have a husband. And you know what she says? 'Do not worry, we have orphanages.'" Nadia exploded stormily. "I have heard stories

43

of these orphanages, Greg. Nightmares! In any case, you believe me – I am not that sort of person!"

It is strange how walking makes it easy to talk of private things. Perhaps because you are side by side, not staring into your companion's face. You can discuss anything.

"I don't know how you put up with it," I said.

"After a while I couldn't. I left the job. But it is the same in all big undertakings. So I had to finish up in the shop. Madame is a real horror, but she does not ask awkward questions. No, not *those* questions," she said with a laugh, seeing that I had misunderstood. "A different problem. By leaving the office I lost my residence-permit – you cannot live in Bucharest without one. The housing shortage – the Comrade has swept away thousands of old houses to make space for his schemes. Of course, people break the regulations, find somewhere to live, change their addressess constantly – they're called 'floaters'."

"And you're a 'floater'?"

"Yes." She laughed again. "You see why I must be careful." She spread her arms expansively. "Oh, it is good to be out here with you and talk freely. I am so *tired* of being always discreet. Not a word against the Party – "

"Or the damned Securitate!"

"You are a poet, Greg."

The sun was going down in one of those scarlet-flaming skies you get in winter. The breeze blew chilly off the water. She took my arm.

"I suppose we ought to turn back," I said. "You must show me somewhere nice to eat." I had made up my mind on one thing. I was going to buy her the best meal we could find in this god-forsaken town.

CHAPTER
FIVE

We walked back into the city. The crowds flowed past us, absorbed in their own concerns. I thought of the very different crowds at home intent on Christmas, shops bright with flashing lights and decorations, children pointing and demanding, everyone weighed down with gift-wrapped packages.

Nothing like that here. The government frowned on religious survivals. Yet even the Comrade could not stamp out deep-seated memories. People kept Christmas alive as best they could, with so little now to buy in the shops. Nadia had heard about the old days from her elders. The markets full of holly and bay and little Christmas trees cut down on the mountainsides of the Carpathians, and the food, such delicacies as were never seen nowadays...

My father admired Ceausescu because he was rare among Communist dictators in paying his

foreign debts. But he paid them by selling the
country's food-production abroad and letting the
people go hungry. Today it was all rationing.
Flour, sugar, cheese, eggs – five eggs a month if
you were lucky. "Even potatoes are scarce," said
Nadia. "Meat is even scarce on the black market!
One has to stand in line – and what time have *I*,
unless Madame sends me out to stand for her?"
She could grumble almost frankly in the street.
Everyone else did. Even the Comrade could not
bug every conversation.

We reached the Calea Victoriei, once the
smart shopping street of Bucharest, now with
its restricted lighting quite literally a shadow of
itself. The restaurants were not serving dinner
yet. "Let's sit down anyhow," I said.

We found a café. I remembered the special
Romanian drink was *tuica*, so I offered her one.
"Is it an aperitif?" I added hesitantly.

"Oh, yes. You like it?"

"I've never tried it."

She smiled. "It is made from plums. A sort
of brandy. Quite powerful."

That worried me slightly. But I said, airily,
"You'll have one?"

"Just now I would prefer coffee. You have
your *tuica*."

"No," I said, "coffee sounds a good idea."

The waiter brought cakes. I caught the look in
her eyes and pressed her to take one. "It won't
spoil your appetite."

She laughed, quite literally a hollow laugh, I
imagine. A sparkle replaced the wistful look. "In

Romania we no longer worry about 'appetite'. We can always rely on hunger." Her upper lip acquired a white moustache of whipped cream. A little pink tongue emerged and licked it off with unashamed pleasure.

We sat for a while in great contentment, then parted briefly to freshen up before going on to the restaurant. When she rejoined me she had run a comb through her windswept hair. She was emphatically a girl to go out with. Her skirt was longer than the girls were wearing at home just then, a pity, because her legs were really good. The Comrade, however, disapproved of decadent Western fashions. If a girl's skirt were too short or a man's hair too long a policeman might stop them in the street and say so.

Nadia was determined not to involve me in outrageous extravagance. She rejected several restaurants. "Perhaps here?" she suggested at last. "I have always wanted to eat here."

The doorman took our top coats. At the table Nadia whispered, "What on earth have you in your pockets? Why do you spoil the shape of that beautiful coat? All men are the same!"

"Just oddments," I said evasively. I meant to hand over my Comturist purchases later. How could *she* have carried them? I studied the menu. "You must explain all this to me."

"The Bucharest black market," she murmured, "is even blacker than most." We settled for a chicken stuffed with smoked bacon, sausage and other powerfully flavoured items. Before that we had dumpling soup and we ended with rum-sweetened pancakes, to which apparently her countrymen were much addicted.

The waiter suggested *tuica* with our coffee, but Nadia shook her head decisively. She was looking rather pink, her eyes even brighter than usual. We had drunk white wine.

"What would you like to do now?" I asked. With our dining early the night was yet young. I wondered half-heartedly about a film.

"That would be a waste of talking time. It is sad your stay in Bucharest is so short."

"They're expecting me in Mayrhofen."

"Of course! I can imagine how much your parents – " She broke off, then resumed, "In any case I shall soon be going to my sister's at Timisoara. But this evening . . ."

"Perhaps we could go to the Carpathia? We could sit in the bar and talk."

I sensed she was uneasy. The restaurant was all right, anonymous. My hotel was different. My name was in the register, my nationality . . . Nadia, in my company, would attract notice. A Romanian forming any acquaintance with a foreigner was supposed to report the fact to the police within twenty-four hours and answer any questions they cared to ask.

"It can be awkward," she whispered, "especially if you are a floater. Better if we went to a disco. You like?"

"Great."

The disco was only a short walk away, in the warren of cobbled byways off the Strada Lipscani, near her shop. It was dark even by local standards, with pallid chinks of gaslight showing through shutters. Booted shadows clumped to and fro over uneven cobbles. Suddenly music throbbed beneath our feet. "This way," said Nadia, steering me through an arch and then a doorway. "Careful on the stairs!"

We groped our way down into a big cellar, the brickwork curving overhead. A massive figure loomed, greeting her by name, a real heavy, like a grizzly on his hind legs, but more benevolent.

"This is Janos," she said. "My cousin Greg – from England."

"Hiya," said the affable grizzly from a great height, seizing our coats in massive paws.

"Three *lei* each," Nadia whispered. I paid the small sum required and we edged our way forward through the cigarette smoke. It was a dense fog, not grey but orange or green or purple as the fumes were caught in the spinning lights. "We can sit here," she said, her breath warm against my ear.

My eyes grew accustomed to the feverish effects of the strobe. There was no band, it was all recorded music, run-of-the-mill stuff, out of date to my ears. There were maybe a hundred people crammed in there, mostly students. I was suddenly reminded of home – the slashed jeans, the single earrings, the T-shirts often with American logos, a couple of gays. But no sign of liquor or syringes, only coffee and soft drinks. Yet the place was obviously popular. It was a respite from all the regimentation elsewhere. Even the pop music was a defiance of the Comrade, George Orwell's Big

Brother made real.

I was conscious that Nadia was studying my face. She smiled and whispered, "The alternative society."

I mouthed my answer silently against the din. "Good luck to it!"

Conversation was hardly possible. We got up and joined the dancers, swaying and whirling, laughing in each other's hot faces, while the lights spun crazily, splashing us with their garish colours, and the insistent rhythm throbbed, banishing thought.

I am not a great one for discos. I tag along with the gang to be sociable. I found myself enjoying this more than most, but it was, like a film, rather a waste of talking time. After an hour Nadia said, "I think you do not much like this music?"

It was not the time to explain. I had nothing against this vibrant sound – it could be a helpful background even for the development of a new friendship – but I just never thought of it as music. She spared me the embarrassment of answering. "Shall we go?" She stood up.

Janos handed us our coats. Out in the fresh night she said, "I have not far to go. So... there is no need. You see where we are?"

"Isn't that the Stavropoleos church over there?"

"Yes. So you know your way from here."

"Sure. But I must see you to your door." I was afraid she might make some excuse. She was – well, not secretive, but a little cagey at times.

No wonder, in this country. But surely by now she trusted *me*?

"Thank you," she said to my relief. "You must notice the turnings. Then, if you can get yourself back to the Stavropoleos, you will be all right." This old quarter of the city was certainly rather a maze.

As we walked I said, "Could we meet again tomorrow?"

"Oh, please! It will be our last chance."

"Then –" I tried to sound casual. "We had better fix something –"

She paused under an archway opening blackly in the wall of the lane. "This is where I live. You'd better come in for a minute." Her key clicked. I stepped after her into a dimly-lit passage, flagged. It looked like – and proved to be – the servants' entrance of what had been a mansion in days gone by, but had gone down in the world and was now rented out as shabby lodgings.

Nadia became almost stealthy, a warning finger on her lips. I thought of sundry past occasions when I had stayed with a friend and it had seemed desirable for some innocent – or relatively innocent – reason not to wake his parents. But Nadia's parents were dead and this was still quite a respectable hour. None the less, we tiptoed and did not speak until another key clicked, and then a light switch, and we were inside her room with the door closed softly behind us.

I saw a cheerless little apartment with a table,

two hard chairs and a divan against the wall. She leapt across to this with an embarrassed gesture, dragging a quilt over her tousled bedding and pyjamas. "I overslept – I did not think I would have a visitor."

"Am I a visitor? A cousin? Surely I'm *family*?"

She laughed, more herself again. "Yes, please – "

I glanced round. In the far corner by the window a wash-basin and tap. A very small, very obsolete gas fire, with a ring beside it, a kettle, saucepan and frying pan. She stooped, a match scraped, the gas popped explosively. The room had been cold and stuffy. It became slightly less cold and very much stuffier. The place was a slum and a potential deathtrap. I concealed my horror and remarked cheerfully, "So this is your little kingdom?"

She shrugged. "It is where I can do as I like. Not a kingdom – but at least an autonomous republic."

At last I could empty my pockets. She cried out. The chocolates delighted her. The coffee beans made her almost delirious. She hugged me.

"Oh, *Gregory*! Thank God I did not throw away my old grinder – though I never dreamt I should have beans again. Do you know what they cost on the black market? Six hundred *lei* for a kilo!"

She must celebrate by giving me real coffee there and then. It would make the perfect ending, she declared, to this wonderful day. She measured out a few beans and began to turn the handle. A new, much preferable smell started to compete with the gas fumes.

It was then that there came an insistent knocking on the door.

CHAPTER SIX

"Now who on earth – ?"

Nadia was really startled.

"Move over there," she whispered hoarsely before she opened the door. I stepped into the corner screening the wash-basin. "Oh, it's you, Sofia." Nadia's tone was one of relief rather than welcome.

The caller was pouring out apologies, a request of some sort. Nadia stemmed the flow decisively.

"I can spare a cupful, but I really must ask you, this time—"

"Of course! Tomorrow without fail!"

Nadia walked across to her cupboard. There was no movement from the waiting unknown outside the door. Not surprisingly. There had been no pressing invitation to come in. Nadia went back. "There you are."

"I am so sorry to have interrupted you."

"Not at all."

The stranger's voice sank to a confidential whisper. "But you have someone with you? I heard voices. . ."

Denials were obviously useless. "My cousin."

"I could have sworn I heard a *foreigner*!"

Nadia laughed unconvincingly. "He was showing off his English – making out it was as good as mine."

I caught no more of their murmured dialogue. The door closed. Nadia stood by it, listening intently, then signalled the all-clear.

"A snake," she said. "It comes of living in a house like this. Floaters cannot be too choosy." Sofia was a nosy neighbour from the end of the passage.

"I don't think she believed it was a cousin – though it was. She had a particularly dirty giggle."

"I did not mean her to believe me," said Nadia surprisingly. "She went away satisfied."

"Satisfied?"

"That I am no better than other girls. That after all I do have young men here. She has evidence now. She had not, before, because there was none." Nadia looked up at me earnestly before she poured the hot water on the coffee. "You believe me, Greg? I am not such a girl."

I remembered her frank speaking in the park. "Sure I believe you!"

We sat down again. That coffee certainly was good. For me it was only the best since Vienna a week or two ago. To judge from Nadia's ecstatic expression it was the best she had tasted in years.

"This is fun, yes?" I nodded vigorously. "I wish you were staying longer," she said.

"So do I."

"You should see more of this country, not only Bucharest." She described Timisoara, where she would be going to her sister's. "It is – different. More western. Of course, it is so close to Hungary – it *was* Hungarian until after the First World War. In those days it was part of the Austrian Empire."

I was hazy about European history. All those complicated boundary changes meant nothing to me, they were not relevant to life as we knew it now. But having recently had my first sight of Vienna and fallen for that magical city, I could imagine that some of its quality might have rubbed off on the smaller places its emperors had once ruled.

As we finished the coffee a power cut came. The feeble gas fire gave enough light for Nadia to find a candle. "It happens all the time," she said. "It is much worse if they cut off the gas. That is frightening."

"I'll say!" I was frightened for her. If she did not check that the taps were turned off, and the supply came on again, in the middle of the night, say, she might never wake again.

The softer light was kind to the room's shabbiness. It was becoming almost cosy. But when I peered at my watch I saw that I must be going. We arranged to meet again by the Stavropoleos.

This time it would be five before she could leave the shop.

She saw me out, the candle flickering in her hand. I must not trip in the dark passage. Outside, the night was clear and starry. With so little street-lighting anyhow, the power cut did not make much difference. Once my eyes were adjusted I could see my way quite well. I had only to concentrate on the turnings.

One thing slightly disturbed me. At first I took little notice of the passers-by. I was just relieved that there were plenty of them. This was not the most respectable quarter of the town and at this late hour I might have felt uneasy in such a maze of insalubrious lanes. No one wants to be mugged, least of all abroad, where the loss of one's wallet and passport can be disastrous. It was good to see so many people still about, but I grew faintly uneasy when I realized that one man, just one, seemed by coincidence to be going my way. Consistently. For all my successive turnings to left or right – and my momentary hesitations at a doubtful corner, when I would have expected him to overtake me and hurry on – he seemed to adjust his pace and keep a constant distance between us.

My fists clenched instinctively. Was I bracing myself to run or to lash out in self-defence? I don't know. Because I'd no idea of what *he* was going to do. Probably nothing, I tried to convince myself.

I was right. The good old Stavropoleos loomed ahead, its little tower unmistakable against the star-pricked sky. I was on familiar ground, I could quicken my step with confidence. I turned along the Strada Lipscani, soon I was in the Calea Victoriei. Plenty of people about. No one would try anything here. Five more minutes brought me to the turning for my hotel. Just then the power came on again, the entrance leapt suddenly to light. I ran up the steps. The night-porter was collecting up the lamps and candlesticks that he had ranged around the foyer. I was heading for the lift when he called out an apologetic warning. It had been caught between two floors and it would be safer to wait till it had been checked and was in normal working order. I had no wish to end my happy day trapped in a lift, so I started up the stairs.

I climbed slowly. It had been a long day and so was each successive flight. I was still within earshot when the sound of my own name came floating up from below. I stopped, my fingers tightening on the handrail, and peered down. In the yellow circle of light round the reception-desk I saw the porter and another man bending over the hotel register. I heard my name again, "Byrne", and "British".

I had never yet had a clear view of the man following me. I knew only that he was not massive – much my own height, which had been reassuring – and that he was wearing a soft hat. So was this one and from the stairs his features were completely concealed. He presumably looked respectable, for the porter was answering his questions with deference. Then the stranger turned on his heel and marched out.

So I had been shadowed. And, from the porter's manner, not by an obvious crook but more likely by a policeman. How long had he been on my tail? I thought back over the evening. Nothing extraordinary about our dining together in the restaurant. We had watched our tongues. I recalled the feeble rhyme we had laughed over in the safety of the empty park.

Not a word against the Party,
Or the damned Securitate!

It did not sound so funny now.

I did not think we had been spied upon in the disco. It was not the kind of place where a Securitate man would have escaped notice himself. I decided that my shadow had most likely been waiting for me outside Nadia's when I left. Which pointed to a simple explanation. The nosy neighbour had not been taken in. Suspicious still, she had picked up a phone and made a report.

Fantastic? A day or two ago I might have said so. Now Nadia had put me wise to a lot of things. The Securitate was a vast organization with tens of thousands of members in uniform and countless others in plain clothes. They had the backing too of innumerable part-time informers – waiters, cab-drivers, janitors, always ready to pass on information they picked up. Half the population of Bucharest, said Nadia, had a link with the Securitate.

It was scary, though I reasoned that I had nothing to fear myself. I had broken no law. But Nadia would do, if she did not report her encounter with me in the next twenty-four hours. I was very doubtful if she meant to. Because of the residence problem she preferred to avoid official contacts.

There was nothing I could do tonight. She had no telephone — even if it were safe to use it. Tomorrow I had better go straight to the shop when it opened, buy something to placate the old woman, and have a message ready written to slip into Nadia's hand when I paid. The warning could not wait till we met later in the day.

I was finding the atmosphere of this city sinister. I felt a sudden yearning for the familiar voices of home. My parents would still be up. I asked the porter to get me the number.

My mother answered. "Greg! How *lovely*! How are you?"

"Fine, Mum, everything's fine."

I had heard sundry clicks. I was pretty sure that a foreign call would be bugged.

She was in the bedroom, she said, sorting out clothes for the winter sports. "And —" she hesitated " — how's Bucharest?"

I would never tell Mum a lie. But I don't always complicate life by telling her everything. "Interesting," I said.

CHAPTER
SEVEN

Next morning it was the other porter on the desk. I craftily asked him how to find the Railway Museum.

"In the Calea Grivitei, out beyond the Gara de Nord. Shall I call you a taxi?"

"Thank you, I'll walk."

He gave me directions. But when I reached the Calea Victoriei I turned south.

The shop seemed surprisingly busy. Nadia and Madame were fairly scuttling around. Rugs were being rolled up, blouses folded, fragile items carefully packed. Nadia spun round, forgetting for an instant to behave like an impersonal saleswoman.

"Good morning," I said, poker-faced and correct. She became the helpful saleswoman again. I murmured something about presents. As before, we conducted a two-level conversation as we rummaged among the stock.

I did not mention my shadower. It was all in the note anyhow. Madame was soon scowling because I had not produced my wallet. She snarled a tart suggestion that Nadia should waste no more time but persuade the young Englishman to buy something and send him on his way.

Nadia could look meek when it suited her. She answered slowly so that I could understand her Romanian. "I was telling the gentleman that he must decide today. That we are closing at midday, until the New Year."

"I'm glad you're showing some enterprise!"

I had got the message. Examining a carved bowl I said, "So you can meet me earlier?"

"Soon after one?"

"Fine. The coffee bar under the square?"

"OK. Fifty *lei*." She put out her hand, pretending we had agreed the price. I pulled out a one-hundred note, folded it round the message I had written, and slipped them both into her hand. She palmed my letter deftly as she walked across to the cash desk.

The circular coffee bar was a good rendezvous, with its patrons constantly changing. When Nadia arrived she did not seem unduly worried by my warning. Perhaps it was a small thing compared with the bad news that Madame was closing for two whole weeks. There were few tourists at this season.

I stared. "You won't get paid?"

"She says, why should she pay me if I am not working?"

63

"But – how will you get by?" I was really concerned.

"I shall go to my sister's for a little longer. I have just telephoned her. She always says her home is mine until I marry. And if now I am to be in trouble about my residence-permit – "

That brought us back to our other worry. Would her contact with me cause serious difficulties? Would she report it?

"No, I'll chance it. For today I am still inside the time-limit. Tomorrow I shall be in the train to Timisoara." She laughed in my face. "Dear Greg! We must not become paranoid. The system is not always too efficient. Life is still possible. I am not a dangerous dissident. I am just a little, little fish. I get by."

"Well," I said gloomily. "I shan't cause you further trouble after today."

"Ah!" She raised a finger in rebuke. "We come now to another question. Demanding quick decision." I looked nervous. "No," she said, "it is something nice – if you agree. *Must* you start for Austria tomorrow?"

I hesitated. "Well – I've worked out a lot of train times – but I suppose I – ".

She tossed her head. "You could rearrange them? You have a few more days to play with. So long as you join your parents at Mayrhofen by Christmas?"

"Well – yes – " My resistance crumbled. Zigzagging about on continental railway routes was fun for the real enthusiast, but she was hinting at a counter attraction.

"Many foreign expresses stop at Timisoara. It could be fitted splendidly into your schedule. There are connections to Belgrade, Budapest, Vienna... I told you, I had just telephoned to Ana. I could not say things too clearly – you know how it is?"

"I should by now!"

"She will be doubly delighted when she learns who is this 'special friend' I wish to bring. Remember, you are her cousin as well as mine. Say you will come!"

It was impossible to refuse. A few days staying with Nadia and her sister seemed far more appealing than a solitary exploration of the railway system in the depths of winter. "Only," I said, "how about these government regulations? Mightn't I land *her* in difficulties?"

"Timisoara is not Bucharest, thank God. Regulations are sometimes forgotten there – or shall we say, 'interpreted'. The rule against foreigners in private homes is to prevent people getting hard currency that way. The government wants to grab all that through its hotels. But I am sure that hospitality between close relatives..."

"How close is 'close'?"

She eyes me rather humorously. "I feel that *we* have become quite close."

"So do I!"

"Then it is settled."

We went straight round to the office of the C.F.R., the Romanian state railways, to make sure of our tickets. It would be best, we decided, if I bought them and she kept in the background. Then, if anyone remembered the young Englishman, they would at least not connect him with a girl.

"Also," said Nadia, "you can go straight to the head of the queue, as you are a foreigner. I should have to wait for hours."

"It's so unfair!"

"Sh. We get used to unfairness. It is simpler to submit. We have a favourite saying in Romania: 'Kiss the hand you cannot bite'." She laughed. "Sometimes, Greg, I am afraid you will explode." She pushed me off into the agency. "Singles," she warned me. "We do not have return tickets. And buy reservations – we do not want to stand for perhaps eight hours."

Reserved seats would have another advantage. We need not attract notice by boarding the train together. We should meet in our numbered seats apparently by accident. The fare seemed extraordinarily reasonable.

I rejoined Nadia unobtrusively. She took her change and her ticket and slipped them into her bag. "And now?" she enquired.

"Comturist!"

"Comturist?"

"Now you're with me we can choose something you really want."

"But you gave me the coffee! And those chocolates!"

I must show her that I too could be firm. "Christmas," I explained, "I'll be far away by then. Let's get something now."

She protested no more. She was round-eyed and

gaping in that Aladdin's cave of hard currency. No shadows of the Securitate darkened that precinct. The sight of English boy and local girl simply meant more hard currency.

As I expected, Nadia was most tempted by everyday items unobtainable, or vastly inferior, in the ordinary stores. She would not let me lavish my money on what was extravagant but useless. "OK," I said, "if that's the way you want it, let's make up a mixed bag."

I would not let her agonize between tights and scented soap. She'd have both. The same with make-up. When she positively refused to accept anything more I made her help me pick something for her sister.

"Ana would adore some of this exquisite soap." She agreed to my adding coffee beans. Josef, my host, was easy. American cigarettes, a big pack of Kents, the brand most desired by Romanians. Nadia suggested I bought some for myself.

"But I don't smoke."

"I know. But they can be so useful. They oil the wheels in awkward situations. Sometimes it is inappropriate to offer money. Nobody refuses American cigarettes. At really tricky moments you hand round the pack and beg them to help themselves."

We were going to have dinner again together. "You are spending too much on me," she protested, "but..." She did not finish the sentence, but I could have done it for her. She could not afford to go Dutch, even if I let her. So I said lightly, "I'm doing this on my mother's behalf, you know that. She'd have something to say if she thought I hadn't treated you properly. I promise – if I need to, I'll put in a claim for expenses when I get home!"

"Most businesslike! Mind you do."

This time Nadia picked a cheaper restaurant, but we enjoyed ourselves. She was looking forward so much to taking me home and showing me another side of her country. It had been a bad start to her day, with the shop closing abruptly and the fear (I guessed) that the job might not be there for her after the New Year. The old hag was quite unpredictable. Now the gloom had lifted. Whatever 1990 might hold, 1989 was going to end on a high note.

Tonight, though, we had better be cautious. I would not take her right home, only as far as the Stavropoleos. Her neighbour might have her ear cocked for a foreign voice and report that the same young man was there again.

Never mind, tomorrow morning we'd be safely in the train, gliding out of this city of eavesdroppers. In Timisoara, Nadia promised, we should not be glancing over our shoulders all the time.

I was at peace with the world when I walked back into my hotel. I stopped short as I crossed the threshold. A familiar voice at reception, one I had heard last night at this same place – a guttural voice that asked questions in the accent of authority, with a faint menace, a voice that waited confidently for an answer and always seemed to get it, however hesitant and apologetic.

"Leaving tomorrow, you say? To where?"

"He did not say. Austria, I think. A morning train. He has asked for his bill to be ready."

I had. There was no doubt that I was the guest under discussion.

A party came streaming in from the street. I took the chance to slip outside again. I was pretty sure that my presence had not been noticed. The desk was some way inside, the conversation had continued unbroken.

I went down the steps and waited in the gloom. I had not long to wait. The next person to emerge was the Securitate agent. For the first time I got a good look at him as he paused in the doorway and took out a cigarette. His face was clear in the lighter-flame. A hard man, forty to fifty. Bushy moustache, eyebrows to match.

He puffed out the first smoke, thrust the lighter into his pocket, and came down the steps. I had retreated further into the shadows and now moved forward again briskly, as though I had just appeared. We passed on the bottom step. He showed no sign of recognition, though we instinctively exchanged glances to avoid colliding. But I felt sure that, with the practised observation of a detective, he had identified me. I dared not look back, but I had caught the sudden break in his footsteps as he did. Then they resumed, steadily receding down the street.

So my shadow had not given up yet, though it was probably mere routine. He had been assigned to this job, he was to keep tabs on the English youth while he remained in town. He would keep at it until he could file his last report and be given another equally useless duty. Whatever my dislike of the Ceausescu regime I could hardly be a serious threat to its survival.

As soon as I unlocked my door I knew that my shadow had not stopped at questioning the porter. I could smell those foul Romanian cigarettes.

It could, of course, have been one of the hotel staff. But I had only to open the first drawer to see that my possessions had been thoroughly gone over.

Especially my papers.

There were no state secrets here, no enigmatic messages in cipher, no stolen plans. Just souvenir concert programmes and menus, letters from Mum and my friends that had caught up with me on the tour – and of course that photocopy of Nadia's original letter.

At least, that *had* been there, for I remembered putting it back carefully after I had thrust it under Nadia's nose as a proof of my identity.

It wasn't there now. I riffled through those papers with increasing dismay. A peppering of cigarette-ash showed that my visitor had done the same. But of that photocopied sheet, opening *Dear Mrs Byrne, I believe we are distant cousins* ..., there was no trace.

CHAPTER
EIGHT

These people were not exactly subtle.

In any spy story I had ever read the enemy agent or whatever would have whipped out a mini-camera, photographed the document, and left no hint of his visit.

Perhaps at this level they had no call to be subtle or to be equipped with expensive cameras. They were not involved in some desperate struggle between superpowers. Ceausescu's concern was merely to dominate his small country of unorganized, frightened people. He merely had to keep them frightened, so that no one would risk plotting against him.

I recalled what Nadia herself had written. *If I gave you an address to reply to I should soon have the Securitate knocking on my door . . .* If they could scare a girl like Nadia I could believe that they had most of the population just where they wanted them.

The more I thought about it, the more scared I became myself – on her account. This policeman now *had* her address. I was more and more certain that his interest in me had started with her inquisitive neighbour. The signature *Nadia* showed that the letter-writer and my companion of last night were the same person. It showed that her visitor had been a relative from abroad, the son of someone with a suspicious secret which could probably be unravelled from old police files. It revealed that she herself had *a dream to travel*. There was enough in that letter to cause my dear cousin a heap of trouble.

I did not sleep too well. I was down early, settling my bill. I could not wait to get out of the place. "I like to be in good time at railway stations," I told the porter grandly. Today I accepted his suggestion of a taxi. He seized my baggage and went down the steps. "Gara de Nord," he told the driver.

As I sat back I recognized a figure on the pavement. Shaggy-browed eyes were watching from beneath a shadowing hat brim. This fellow was leaving nothing to chance. Or was he? Would he tail me to the station? It hardly mattered if he did. I was taking one of the international expresses to the West, leaving Bucharest as announced, off his patch, no longer his responsibility. The taxi-man drove off and, turning to glance back, I was relieved to see that the man was walking away across the street at a leisurely pace. Within a few minutes we were at the station, a porter was opening the door and demanding my destination.

"Coffee," I said briefly. I was not going

to reveal more until the cab had driven away.

The porter picked up my bag and led me to the buffet. I was in good time, so I paid him off. I would find the train myself. Until I was out of Bucharest I meant to cover my tracks carefully. I would become just one more nameless young tourist, exploring Europe on the cheap. The porter went off quite happily, realizing that there was not much to be made out of my sort.

I sipped my coffee with distaste and surveyed the bustle around me. There was something comfortingly anonymous about the station. Hordes of strangers were in endless motion, arriving, departing and meeting friends. Nadia had told me that economical travellers used stations for free overnight shelter, saving the cost of a hotel. At the Gara de Nord the long-distance international trains were backing in and out at all hours for Belgrade or Budapest or the Black Sea resorts.

Just one face I recognized. An elderly man at a table in the corner, immersed in a book. Where had I seen him before? Take a grip of yourself, I thought firmly. Nadia had warned me not to get paranoid. Even in a city this size you were liable occasionally to see the same individual again. You would be crazy to conclude that he was shadowing you. He could just as reasonably suspect that you were shadowing *him*. I suddenly remembered I had first noticed him at the ticket office yesterday. He'd been reading the same book. I could not see what it was, for it had a protective brown-paper cover.

Then, as now, he showed no interest either in me or his surroundings. What more natural than to see him again at the station this morning?

The final half-hour crept by. I scanned the drifting flow of faces, hoping for a glimpse of Nadia's distinctive mane, reminding myself that we were not to accost each other. She seemed too well organized a person to miss trains, especially this one – unless some last-minute hitch prevented her. Paranoia set in again when I thought back to last night's disappearance of the photocopy. Were the Securitate already hammering on her door?

There you go again, I reflected crossly. Too many spy stories. But I should feel a lot happier when my cousin was beside me in the train, and the suburbs gliding past the window.

I must stay here no longer. The train might be standing ready, she might be sitting in her seat, worrying in turn about *me*. I stood up. The man at the corner table did not raise his bald head out of the book.

The train was in, though not due to leave for almost twenty minutes. Passengers were climbing aboard. Others still stood around, chatting with the friends who were seeing them off. I took out my ticket, glanced at the number of the car, and walked over to it. Now the seat-number... Half the seats were already occupied. I found my own reservation, the one beside it empty, waiting for Nadia. A middle-aged Romanian couple, cluttered with bulging bags, sat facing me.

I studied my watch, licked my dry lips. What if she did not come? Stop, I told myself, you *are* getting paranoid. There are still seven minutes to go.

Someone was coming down the car. The couple opposite drew in their feet politely. But it was not Nadia. It was the bald elderly man with the paper-covered book. He shuffled carefully past the couple and sank into the vacant seat beyond them. His eyebrows went up, imperceptibly, as he identified me. Then he was reading again with his usual concentration.

I had ceased to worry about him. I was concerned only with Nadia's non-appearance. Only four minutes now... Last messages, last embraces were being exchanged outside, in all the chattering voices there was a farewell ring. Laughter, shouts, people clambering aboard, pushing to their seats...

And – at last – Nadia. A wave of relief swept over me. It was an effort not to seek her eyes and signal a greeting. I had to stare straight in front of me and not move a muscle. She was equally discreet. Her eyes slid to the number of the seat beside me, she sat down, pulled off her headscarf, shook out her hair. She must have washed it last night, for it gave off a faint, very attractive fragrance. I smiled inwardly. She had not been able to wait before trying what I had bought her at the Comturist shop.

The station buildings slid behind us. Concrete crates of workers' dwellings rose dirty-white against the sky. I glanced amiably round my fellow-passengers. "Does anyone speak English?" I enquired.

There were shrugged shoulders and apologetic

mumbles. The elderly man merely raised his pale eyes from his book, considering me, and resumed his reading without any sign of comprehension. At last, satisfied that no one else was offering, Nadia said modestly, "I do – a little. Can I help you?"

After that it was all plain sailing. I made some fatuous enquiry about the destination of the train, and then, the ice broken, it was natural we should continue the conversation, though (as in the shop) with the air of strangers.

It was not too difficult. We talked much as we should have anyhow, Nadia pointed out things from the window, I asked questions because I really was keen to learn more of Mum's native country. I did not mention the theft of the photocopy. It would have spoilt our journey. It could wait until we were alone. If anything had happened at Nadia's she would not have been on this train.

The morning brightened. The grey smog of Bucharest gave place to a blue sky. To our right we had, for long stretches, the far-away panorama of the Transylvanian Alps I had seen from the capital. They ran most of the way across the country, walling the north off from the south. Through the left-hand windows we could see the vast plains rolling down to the unseen Danube. Nadia told me how beautiful it was at other seasons – the orchards clouds of blossom, the grape-pickers busy among the vineyards, the ripening corn a giant golden-brown rug over the land.

We finally touched the Danube, which had mostly been miles away to the south. Then it had marked the frontier of Bulgaria. From now onwards, Nadia explained, the opposite bank was Yugoslavia. "Sometimes," she dropped her voice, "people who wish to visit over there, but find it . . . difficult to comply with the regulations. . ."

"They can't get passports?"

She nodded. "They . . . take a little swim."

I remembered the wide Danube I had seen at Vienna and Budapest. Here, hundreds of miles further down stream, it would be wider still. "Not such a 'little' swim," I said.

"No. And the currents are very fast, very dangerous. Perhaps your mother would have been strong enough. I should not like to try."

I wondered if she had ever seriously considered it. Perhaps in time of desperate depression? I was thankful that she had not risked it.

"Also," she went on, "there are the frontier guards – on both banks. They are very ready to shoot." She glanced round, growing bolder. Except for the old man all our nearest fellow-passengers had got out and no one else had got in. Even he had carefully slipped a marker into his book, laid it on his seat, and drifted off down the train. "Often the Yugoslavs send back people they catch," she whispered disgustedly, "and then it is not at all pleasant for them. It is bad luck, if you have escaped drowning, and the bullets – and then –" She paused significantly. "Let's not talk more of such things." She looked across at the book on the vacated seat opposite. "I would love to know what he is reading, that interests him so much!"

"He's a funny old guy. I had my doubts about him at first – he was in the ticket office yesterday – then he turns up on *our* train, sitting opposite..."

"But naturally – it was the next ticket. Innocent enough."

"Of course. Stupid of me."

'I wonder if his book is so innocent," she said wickedly, "or does it contain improper pictures? He covers it so discreetly with brown paper."

I challenged her. "Take a peek then!"

"Oh, I dare not. It would not be polite. But – *you* do."

That put me on the spot. "OK," I said as coolly as I could and stretched out my arm. Then I heard a dry little cough and my hand whipped back like a rattlesnake.

Our fellow passenger settled himself down again, opened his book and spread it on his lap while he polished his spectacles. I had a clear view of the pages, though I could not read the print upside down or even guess at the language. But the figures in the illustration, which he made no attempt to cover, were unmistakably female. They seemed, however, to be most properly clothed in long flowing robes of the richest blue and scarlet and green, with circles of shining gold around each head as a guarantee of more than mere respectability.

The stranger surveyed the empty seats and spoke for the first time, in hesitant but precise English, with what sounded like a French accent.

"So, they have departed, the others? So now, my children, you need no longer act a comedy. You are not, unless I am much mistaken, meeting for the first time?"

CHAPTER
NINE

We stared at him. Nadia began to laugh.

"You *do* speak English," I said accusingly.

"Badly. I did not wish to show how badly – you might ask something I could not answer. An old man's vanity! Also," he added with a smile, "when the young lady volunteered I thought that you would prefer to talk with her." His smile widened to a frog-like grin.

"And you had your book," said Nadia, "Your *so* interesting book!"

"Ah, yes, my book! It is not valuable, but it is scarce. Out of print, like all the best books now. It is very battered, so I take care of it."

He held it out, turning the pages to display the colour plates. It was in French, a book on Byzantine art, mosaics, icons and so forth. He began to describe his tour of the famous painted churches.

It was getting dark by now. The pallid bulbs

of the train shed too feeble a light for him to go on reading, and he seemed happy to talk. When his English faltered Nadia helped out by dropping into French. No wonder the old hag found her useful.

"We're getting near," she said, pointing through the left-hand window. "Those lights on the hill." They seemed to be suspended in the sky. "That's the *old* Timisoara. There was a castle once up there. I show you, tomorrow."

"Always in history this region was a battle-ground," said the Frenchman.

The train began to slacken speed, gliding past factories and apartment-blocks. This looked a sizeable industrial town, with glaring furnaces and the gleaming rails of marshalling yards. Behind, the mass of the old quarter loomed dimly, its lights strung down the steeply climbing streets. The Frenchman was checking his papers methodically, his passport, his receipts for changed currency. He would be crossing the frontier in an hour or two.

With an apologetic smile he held out to me a little wad of crumpled notes. "You will not be offended, my young friend? I cannot take these *lei* out of Romania, they will only be confiscated at the border. I would be so much happier to think of you two sitting in some café, perhaps drinking my health – "

"We'll certainly do that, sir!" The money did not amount to much, but when you are travelling you can always use a little extra. It would have hurt his feelings if I'd refused. And it would have been a shameful waste to let the frontier officials lay their fingers on it.

"You are a dear, monsieur!" Nadia bent down and kissed his cheek. From the old man's face he seemed well satisfied with the exchange.

We pulled into the station, another Gara de Nord, and he waved us on our way with another frog-like grin. We found a taxi and were soon bowling along a broad boulevard. Nadia's sister lived in an eight-storey apartment-block not far away.

"They are lucky," said Nadia. "They are only on the second floor. But we might risk the lift. At least there is no power cut." We sailed up without misadventure. Josef had a good flat, she explained. He was a skilled worker at the big petro-chemical plant and was careful to give no offence to the authorities. "What is your saying, Greg? He 'keeps his nose clean'."

Very wise, I thought, in this country.

We rang the bell. It was Ana who opened the door. There were tempestuous exclamations and ecstatic embraces between the sisters. I took the chance to bring in our bags and close the door. Better if the introductions were made inside.

The girls detached themselves, laughing and chattering incoherently. Ana was rather like her sister but less delicate in feature. Much the same height, but not so slim. I at once saw why.

She took my hand. "And this is your — friend?" Warm and welcoming, but with the protective concern of an elder sister.

"This is Greg." Nadia glanced round to check

that the door was shut. "You must speak slowly – his Romanian is not so good yet. But he is improving. He is Cousin Maria's son."

Ana gaped. "No! From England?"

"From England," I admitted. "It is wonderful to meet you, Ana." It seemed appropriate to kiss.

"It was too involved to explain on the telephone," said Nadia. "Better perhaps to make it a pleasant surprise."

"Much better." Ana's agreement was curiously emphatic. I came to understand why.

A convenient interruption eased the momentary awkwardness. A small boy appeared and hurled himself at Nadia like a human missile.

"Pavel! You are bigger every time I come!"

"Of course." He twisted round in her arms, met my eye, and seized with shyness buried his red face between her breasts. Nadia smiled across his tousled head.

"My nephew Pavel. Three, aren't you?"

"Three and a quarter!"

She set him down. He raced off into the living-room, shouting. Ana herded us after him.

The first face I saw was one that had become all too familiar in the last few days. Nicolae Ceausescu challenged one from posters everywhere. Here too he was on the wall, but as a framed photograph above the supper-table.

"You are welcome," said Josef, rising from the couch. He laid down his newspaper. On its front page, too, was the Comrade's photograph, looking somewhat disgruntled at being set aside in my favour.

Anna was guarded in explaining me. She said only that I had come from Bucharest, with no mention of England. She referred to my mother, but his eyes did not kindle with any curiosity. I wondered how much he knew about that discreditable branch of the family tree. It was past the usual time for the evening meal but Ana apologized for a further brief delay. "Your train was so punctual."

"Of course," said Josef sternly. He grew stiffer when the food was served, instead of warming up as people normally do. Inevitably my English origin could not be concealed. My limited command of Romanian had to be explained. He was relieved, I felt, to learn that I was leaving the country within a few days. I explained how the concert tour had brought me here in the first place. He seemed really impressed when I described the honour paid to us by the Ceausescus. "It is something," he assured me, "that you will remember with pride for the rest of your life."

I agreed that the Comrade President had left me with an unforgettable impression.

Ana felt it safe now to ask about my parents, though she skated round the circumstances that had led her cousin to marry abroad and settle there. From time to time Josef tried to ask me questions, choosing his words with ponderous deliberation to help my understanding, but always she would jump in nervously and answer for me.

"You forget, Josef! Greg does not understand our language well . . ."

"Your cousin should have taught him.

He should be proud of his Romanian blood."

"Oh, I am sure he is. Tell me, Greg," she said brightly. "Will you be a musician? It is important to you? You must be good."

"I – I don't know, Ana." I honestly didn't. Had I any real talent – the real dedication to make a success of it? It was something I had got to find out.

At that point in my life I was more mixed up than I had ever felt before. Was I British, as my passport said, and as school and home surroundings had shaped me? Or did I partly belong, through my mother, to this unknown country I was just discovering? I was confused about nationality and what I wanted to do in life, and in this past week I had become increasingly unsettled in other ways.

Mercifully we did not make too long an evening of it. Josef had to clock in at the plant by half past six. Ana was not due at her textile mill until seven, but she had to deliver Pavel to the kindergarten first. When I showed sympathy Josef was immediately up in arms. They both enjoyed excellent working conditions. The early start was balanced by finishing mid-afternoon. They had one Saturday off in four. Ana would soon be getting generous maternity leave, lazing about in the spring sunshine. Ana interjected mildly that having a baby was not unrelieved fun. Josef patted her encouragingly. "This time, mark my words, things will go better."

That was my first hint that, as Nadia told me

later, they had lost a second child, born after Pavel, and that Ana had been slow to recover. But Josef insisted that she must persevere and fulfil her patriotic quota. So there should be two more babies after this one. "All must do their duty to the State," Josef declared. "The Comrade President expects—"

"The Comrade President may expect," Nadia commented, "but he can never be an expectant mother. Oh, that Josef," she admitted to me privately, "sometimes I want to slap his smug face."

Pavel was put to bed in his parents' room. Josef enjoyed a final cigarette – he was delighted with the present I had brought him and clearly liked something that came out of the West. Ana set the table for breakfast, Nadia came in with a great flapping of clean sheets, which she spread and straightened on the couch with pillows and blankets. This apartment was the cosiest place I had so far met with in Romania.

Josef stubbed out his cigarette and went. "Good night," said Ana. "Sleep well." Nadia stole back, whispered, "Good night, Greg," and crept away. I was left alone with Ceausescu looking down upon me from the wall. I undressed under that chilling gaze, opened the window to clear the smoke, and then reluctantly closed it again. I might be unpopular if Josef and Ana came in for their early breakfast and found the room ice-cold. It was good of them to put up with all this inconvenience on my behalf. I switched off the light, glad to escape the Comrade's baleful gaze, and snuggled down.

I did not fall asleep at once as I had expected. In the silent darkness I was aware of voices in dispute on the other side of the wall.

"Nadia is not a foolish girl." Ana was fiercely defensive.

"It was foolish to bring him here."

"It is only for a day or two."

"Much harm can be done in a day or two."

I pulled the bedclothes over my ears, trying not to listen. When I came up for air they were still at it. Much of their talk I could not catch. Enough for my conscience to tell me I should not eavesdrop. Enough for my curiosity to overcome my conscience.

"You worry too much, Josef." Ana was getting edgy. She'd had a hard day at the mill and in a few hours another would be starting. She had Pavel to look after, she was pregnant, she had prepared a good meal at short notice, she wanted to enjoy her sister's homecoming. "If that is how you feel," she went on, "you had better comply with your blessed regulations. Report that your wife's cousin has turned up from England. The Party can't blame *you*. You didn't invite him."

Josef was not happy. I could tell that from his peevish tone. It was unwise to have relatives in the West.

"Then say nothing. Take a chance — for once in your life."

"If I say nothing, and they find out, it will be much worse. It may leave a suspicion."

"But what can they *do*, for heaven's sake?"

"You will never understand. They do not have

to *do* anything. These things leave a stigma. The word goes round, perhaps I am not completely reliable, perhaps it would be safer to choose someone else. Anything can be affected – a place on the committee, promotion at the plant, our chance of a better flat—"

"I don't want a better flat if we have to crawl for it," said Ana wearily. "But you must make your own decision. Now let me get some sleep."

Josef's querulous voice rumbled on for some time. He liked to justify himself. How accurate Nadia had been when she said that he was a man who liked to keep his nose clean!

At last his grumblings tailed away. Soon I too was asleep.

CHAPTER
TEN

Pipes were clunking and gurgling. My considerate hostess might be creeping about on tiptoe but the bathroom plumbing had no such consideration. I squinted at the luminous face of my watch. Five forty-five. The door opened, the light brutally clicked on. Josef marched in, Ana whispering apologies behind him. He silenced her. "Your cousin will forgive us! We cannot eat in the dark."

"I was not asleep," I said politely. "I am sorry to be a nuisance."

"You are not," Ana assured me. "If only we had another room for guests! But there is a housing shortage – "

Josef, of course, had to correct her. "It is under control." He sat down and began to butter a piece of bread. "But the government cannot plan for every casual visitor."

"Of course not," I said. I could hardly pretend to

go to sleep again. It would have deceived nobody. I lay on my back and the Comrade's portrait looked down on me disapprovingly from the wall.

Josef and Ana ate in silence with practised speed. Ana smiled across at me. "Would you like a cup of tea now? Nadia will make coffee for your breakfast."

I accepted the tea gratefully. I guessed it would make her feel better. It certainly did me. Ana brought in a sleepy Pavel and somehow managed, simultaneously, to ply him with a mug of warm milk, bundle him into his outdoor clothes, and swallow the last mouthful of her own breakfast. In a few minutes they were on their way, Josef turning back only to switch off the light. Whether this was out of consideration for me, or for the conservation of the national power resources, I was not sure.

Further sleep was unlikely. Nadia might sleep on for hours and probably needed to. I must try not to wake her. But it seemed a good idea to get washed while the bathroom was vacant, so I crept there and made as little noise as I could. Feeling much better I returned, dressed and folded my bedding. All this time I was unpleasantly conscious of the Comrade's eyes. Finally I was driven to lift the portrait from its hook and replace it face to the wall.

It would be nice when Nadia woke up. It would be nice to have something to eat. There was a hopeful chink of grey at the window. I was able to dispense with that forlorn little bulb dangling from the ceiling.

The room faced east and soon the sky was turning red.

Something fresh to look at, anyhow. Across the wide boulevard and the river embankment beyond, an expanse of frosty park stretched to the foot of the hill on which the ancient castle had once stood. The high-pitched roofs and belfries still clustered there in picturesque silhouette.

Timisoara was fully awake, traffic streaming, thousands of people trudging to work. The paths slanting up to the old quarter fairly crawling with dark ant-like figures.

Encouraging noises came from the bathroom. Then the living-room door opened and Nadia smiled blearily from a halo of unkempt hair.

"Hi!"

"Hi," I said warmly.

"Slept well?"

"Fine."

She saw the back of the Comrade's photograph and let out a little gurgly laugh. "Naughty!"

I sprang to reverse it. "Sorry — "

"No, leave it — for now. He looks better from the backside."

It was not the moment to correct her English.

"You are dressed," she said, "so you must be ready to eat?"

"We - ell . . ."

"I too! So — if you will excuse my appearance?"

I rather liked her appearance. She had a long brown wrap with an inch or two of pyjama'd ankle flickering about below. I leant against the doorway of the tiny kitchen while she ground the coffee. "This is what you gave *me*," she said. "I will not open Ana's. So . . . we shall have our breakfast. *Then* I will take my bath – with those other beautiful things you bought me. It would be a shame to hurry. I wish to savour!"

I was unwilling to cast a shadow on the day, but I had still not told her about the searching of my hotel room. Now, over our breakfast, with the sun slanting down across the table, I told her about the disappearance of that photocopy.

She considered. "So. They know that the girl in the shop, who met the British boy afterwards, has some kind of family connection with him. But I remember how carefully I worded my letter, in case it fell into the wrong hands. There was nothing political in it. And in your own papers, that this man looked at, there was nothing they could object to?"

"Not a word."

"It is not an offence to have relatives abroad. Who perhaps went long before the Comrade came to power."

"Maybe. But remember, my mother defected."

"I wrote to her only as 'Mrs Byrne'," Nadia reminded me. "Do not worry, Greg. I know they have their files – but this was twenty years ago, before we were born!"

"You're telling me again not to get paranoid."

She laid her hand on mine. "You're not used to living in a country like this – watching your step, having security men shadow you, go through your things. . ."

"I certainly am not."

"Don't imagine *I* enjoy it. Sometimes I have wild dreams of getting away." She spoke with such intensity, the words remained vivid in my memory. "One has to keep one's sanity." She recovered her lighter tone. "They've got nothing on me – except that I've no permit to live in Bucharest. And there are thousands of floaters like me. They've nothing at all on *you*. You've a British passport, you're too young for a spy, they know why you came here, they can check. Anyhow –" she flung out her hands in an expansive gesture – "we're in Timisoara now, where life isn't lived like a melodrama, Timisoara 'the city of gardens'! The sun's shining and I'm going to show you round. But first my bath – and I'll be smelling like a garden myself when you see me again."

And an hour later that was just what she was.

She was in jeans by then, more like a girl back home. In Bucharest I'd seen her only in a dress or a skirt, the way Madame liked her to look when serving customers. She had combed her hair. The smooth mane did not suggest a lion but a well-groomed horse, and the jeans gave her a leggy look to match.

It was good to be out of the apartment. I liked Ana, but Josef was rather a creep.

"He is not, I think, a keen Communist," Nadia explained, when we had dodged over a boulevard and across one of the river-bridges into the park beyond. "He is just careful to conform. He's a Party member because it's safer."

"He's not all that keen on having me here?"

"Oh. . ." She was too honest to deny it. "He's perhaps a little nervous. He's a timid man."

We walked across level ground, reclaimed from the marshes, when the river, the Bega, was made navigable to the Danube. We passed a big Orthodox cathedral, rather pretty with its candle-snuffer tower and little pinnacles, its pale blue patterning and shiny gold. Further on, mounting towards the old quarter, there were Timisoara's famous gardens, laid out where the fortifications had once been.

Only part of the medieval castle survived, a museum now. Most of this inner city had been rebuilt and laid out in the palmy days of the Austrian Empire and I could somehow identify with it more closely. It conjured up the lost world of Mozart and Haydn, Beethoven and Schubert, whose music I had been hearing and playing ever since I could remember. Even this place had its opera house still and three theatres. Three theatres for a town of this size seemed a generous allowance, but when I saw two more cathedrals besides the one we had already passed – one for Roman Catholics in the Austrian baroque style and another for the Serbian Orthodox – it seemed almost excessive.

"We have many religious faiths," said Nadia. "If you don't understand that, you don't understand our country."

Timisoara certainly attracted me more than Bucharest. We strolled through well-laid-out

94

streets and squares, with pollarded trees in trim rows. The houses stood tall, with curly gables and high-pitched roofs and balconies. They were painted in soft colours, pinks and creams, greys and biscuit-browns. The opera square had a great circular fountain where pigeons splashed and fluttered. There were statues of dolphins round the Artesian Well. The Serbian Orthodox bishop had an impressive palace in grey and white stone.

Looking eastwards, through occasional gaps between buildings, I caught glimpses of the mountains, their tops dappled with the first December snows. A great expanse of woodland stretched towards them from the outer suburbs.

"That's the Green Forest," said Nadia. "It is beautiful in the summer. Perhaps tomorrow – if you felt like a walk – "

"Great."

For today we decided to take a light lunch in the old quarter. Ana finished work at three, picked up Pavel, and did her shopping on the way home. She always cooked a good meal for Josef and, Nadia warned me, would make an extra effort in my honour.

Near the Serbian cathedral was the only surviving stretch of fortifications. It was called the Bastion and housed a wine bar and patisserie. We spent a pleasant hour there. As we were leaving we almost bumped into a silver-haired little man carrying – what naturally aroused my interest – a shabby violin-case. He stepped back politely for Nadia, then his sallow face lit up as though switched on.

"Nadia! My dear!"

"Uncle Sandor!"

Her arms wrapped round him. He gasped and chuckled. "My dear, you will crack my ribs! At my age the bones are brittle."

"At your age? But you are immortal. You *must* be immortal! I insist. It is vital to my happiness."

She released him and introduced us. "My cousin, Gregory Byrne, from England – Mr Kadas. Uncle Sandor, I call him – but we are not really related, so I am afraid, Greg, that he is not also *your* Uncle Sandor –"

He shook my hand. "Any cousin of Nadia's is a nephew of mine," he said gravely.

"Greg also plays the fiddle," she told him.

"Yes?" His delight seemed genuine.

"With a youth orchestra in England. He has just been playing in Bucharest. At the Athenaeum!"

"Only in the second violins," I said hastily.

He brushed aside my attempt at modesty. "No matter, my boy. *I* play in the orchestra at our opera house."

"He's the leader," she said.

"We must celebrate." He laid a brown-speckled hand on my sleeve. "We are colleagues, you and I." He shepherded us back into the wine bar and brought us little glasses of *tuica*. The plum brandy still further warmed the atmosphere. "This is an international conference of musicians!" he announced. His questions flowed. Where else had our tour taken us? What were our programmes? "And you see the world," he cried enviously. "You know it is forty years since I was in Vienna? Never have I seen London! Never America!"

He took us round to his flat. "It is very small," he said apologetically as he led us up the winding stairs, "but it is handy for the opera house."

"It's big enough for you," said Nadia, "all on your own."

"But not for a grand piano."

He was determined that I should play and would have liked to provide an accompaniment. He took out his violin and tuned it. I was relieved to see that it was not some treasured instrument of great age and incredible value. I was nervous enough already. I was wondering what little practice pieces I could offer, unaccompanied and without my music. This old man looked as though he had been playing since time began.

"You will give us this pleasure?" he said. "You will let me hear what you can do?" His gentle kindness steadied my nerve. The sense of control came back as I tucked the fiddle under my chin.

I played a favourite bit of Beethoven, the *Romance in F*. Our eyes met. His twinkled encouragement. "Schubert?" I suggested diffidently. He nodded, and I plunged more confidently into a familiar air. The silver-grey head moved contentedly in time with the music, which he must have known backwards.

"You have been well taught," he said when I finished. "Without technique, nothing. For the rest –" he spread his hands – "time will show."

97

A courteous but honest comment. I was relieved that there were no empty compliments. He was not pretending to have noted any great promise, much less recognized future genius. I think I knew in my heart by this time I was not bad, but I would never be that good.

"Will you play us something yourself, Uncle Sandor?" said Nadia.

He took back the violin. With a seraphic smile he played some Bach. Then, "Memories of the orchestra pit!" he announced with a chuckle, and plunged impromptu into a sequence of operatic airs. The fiddle sang like a human voice. Mozart, Verdi, Puccini — he whipped from one composer to another. I think I recognized them all. Naturally they were from the popular operas that would be regularly in the repertory.

When at last he paused Nadia said, "Will you play Greg some of that country music I loved as a little girl? What you played for the dancing at village weddings and..."

"The folk music?" His face clouded. "I never play it now."

"Never?" she echoed, mystified and dismayed.

"It is two years since I played such music."

Suddenly the atmosphere in the little room was tense. I stared from one to the other, anxious to miss nothing.

"It was outside the city," he went on, "but someone telephoned the Securitate. They came racing out in their cars. They ordered us to stop. We protested. They beat us up."

She cried out in horror. "But why?"

98

"That folk music is Hungarian, it belongs to the old days, that is why people love it. But it does not fit in with the Comrade's vision of a greater Romania." He spoke the last words with infinite contempt. "Everything that reminds people here of Hungary is discouraged. They warned me never to play such music again."

"Not even here? In your own room?"

"I have neighbours. My neighbours have telephones. And the Securitate respond promptly to the telephone. So . . . you will excuse me?" He looked terribly distressed. "I must seem to you a very timid old man."

"Heavens, no!" she protested. "We wouldn't want to get you into trouble. You say they beat you up? They'd do that again? A man of *your* age?"

"Worse, actually." He spoke with measured calm. "I recall exactly what the officer said. 'If you play such music again it will be the last that you play – ever. We shall simply break your fingers.'" Uncle Sandor made an apologetic gesture. "You can imagine, my dear, what that would mean to me."

She nodded dumbly. So, even here, I thought with bitter revulsion, we had not escaped the shadow of the Securitate.

CHAPTER
ELEVEN

Nadia found her voice again. "I can scarcely believe this. You – who are so respected. The leader of the orchestra. They beat you up. And make this threat – "

"Last month they beat up my young friend Lazlo Tokes – a minister of religion, the pastor of the Hungarian Reformed Church – "

I pricked up my ears. Hungarian again. But a clergyman. This would be something to tell Holy Joe when I got home.

"Four masked men broke into his flat," said Uncle Sandor. "He's a big fellow, powerful, but he hadn't a chance – they had clubs and knives. They got him down on the floor. There were ordinary police in the street outside – his wife screamed to them for help. They were not interested. They'd been watching the flat for months. They did not lift a finger."

"Why were they watching the flat?" I asked.

He turned to answer me. "Lazlo's been on their black list for ages. He used to be at Dej before. He won a name for preaching dangerous sermons." The old man smiled. "He was ingenious. He'd take his text from the Book of Kings — safe enough! All about the misdeeds of King Nebuchadnezzar of Babylon. Only the whole congregation knew he meant 'the Comrade'."

"Crafty!" This, I thought, would appeal to Joe.

"But the authorities realized why his church was always full. They had him transferred here in disgrace, to be just an assistant to the old minister. The same thing happened. Always a full attendance if he was preaching. Then the pastor died — and there was such a popular demand for Lazlo that the Bishop had to yield to it and give him the post. Lazlo became more and more outspoken. He denounced systemization — "

"That's the government's policy of sweeping away the old villages," Nadia interjected for my benefit. "Shifting the peasants into these hideous concrete blocks."

"Last summer he went too far," Uncle Sandor continued. "He gave an interview to a Canadian television team. It was broadcast in the Hungarian *Panorama* programme. Plenty of people here can get that programme. The fat was in the fire."

"I should think so." Nadia's tone was mixed anxiety and delight.

"Lazlo was already under suspension. The Bishop is spineless — terrified of the government. Now he's transferred him to Mineu."

101

"*Mineu?* It's only a one-horse hamlet. There's only a cart-track to Mineu — if anyone wanted to go there."

"Lazlo certainly doesn't. He's refused point-blank."

"Can he?" I asked.

'He's under an eviction order, but he won't budge. His flat is in the same building as his church — just a floor below it. So he does not have to go outside. It's a state of siege. There's been so much publicity, it's got into the foreign press. The police don't want more publicity by breaking in for a second time."

"They'll find some way," Nadia prophesied gloomily.

It was time for us to go. Ana would be leaving work and we must not upset her routine. What with her job and the housekeeping, Pavel to look after and the unborn child she was carrying, she deserved all our consideration.

"I'll walk with you," said Uncle Sandor. "I want to look in on Lazlo."

We walked down across the park in the gathering dusk. The boulevard beyond the river was beaded golden with the lights of the home-going traffic. "You should have seen those embankments just two years ago," he murmured. "There had been a great strike at Brasov. Ten thousand workers demanding their back pay, protesting against redundancies. They wrecked the Party offices. It looked as though the worm was turning at last. We had a demonstration of sympathy here, people marched along the embankments singing

'Awake, Romania!' But it came to nothing. The Securitate clamped down at Brasov. Things went on just as before."

"Will they always?" said Nadia. The despair persisted in her voice.

We crossed the river to the boulevard. She said we were getting near the Hungarian church. "Listen! Can you hear that singing?"

The deep voices rang clear and measured through the darkness, disciplined as a choir. Some of the passers-by were quickening their pace. "It's at Lazlo's," panted Uncle Sandor.

The pavement ahead was thronged. People flowed off the kerb. The traffic had to slow. The singing was powerful, resonant, defiant. An old gentleman greeted Uncle Sandor by name, almost ceremoniously. The crowd in general was noticeably respectable. There was no mob.

"What is happening?" Uncle Sandor asked.

"We are picketing to defend the pastor. The eviction order came into force today. He still refuses to move out. They sent thugs to smash his windows – he has boarded them up. The word has gone round. First, his own people rallied. Then, as you see, others like myself. As you know, I am no Hungarian, this church is nothing to me, but I respect the pastor – and I respect freedom of speech. So –" the old gentleman laughed almost apologetically – "I picket. Even I!"

I heard Nadia murmur, "Good for you!"

The singing paused. We edged forward. Uncle Sandor was a well-known figure and people moved aside to let us through. Some greeted

Nadia and eyed me with interest. "They are only disappointed," she whispered, "that you don't look old enough to be a journalist. But anyone from the West is welcome."

The pastor had just finished boarding up his windows. He was a tall, clean-shaven young man in an apron. The hand he thrust out was big and workmanlike, a strong hand.

"From England? Excellent. Tell them what you see here."

I promised I would.

"So you are preparing for a siege?" said Uncle Sandor.

"I am."

"This is no place for your wife in her condition. Or your little boy."

"Edit has taken him to his grandmother's. But she says a wife's place is with her husband."

Some men from the picket came up. Reluctantly Nadia and I slipped away. We must not be late back. As we walked briskly along she had a sudden thought. "Did you put back the portrait the proper way?"

I looked at her aghast. "Oh, Lord! I don't think I did!"

"We must just hope that Josef hasn't got back before us." She did not sound too confident.

It was with some relief that we met him at the lift. But once we got inside the flat, I thought, we might have to be quick and crafty. As we waited for the lift he asked a polite question about our day, which we answered mechanically. But then his question had been itself mechanical. True politeness was not his natural characteristic. If it had been, he might have stood aside when he opened the door of the flat and let Nadia enter before him – me too, even, as a guest. So, if Ana had not reached home before him, we'd have had those extra seconds to put things right.

No such luck. Josef was so used to thinking of himself as head of the family that he marched through that door as though by natural right – and straight on into the living-room.

I had just a split second to register, with relief, the fact that Ana and Pavel were already back – and to pray fervently that she had been into that room and noticed the picture – when the relief was shattered by Josef's shout, "What are you doing with that?"

Nadia and I exchanged glances of despair. His cry could refer to only one thing.

Ana's voice was meek and submissive. "It looked a little dusty – I thought, that will never do."

"I should think not!"

As I entered the room my eye met the cold stare of the Comrade from his usual place of honour. Ana's hands were still uplifted, straightening the picture precisely on the wall. It was well, I thought, that photographs could not speak or their eyes flicker to reveal their feelings.

Ana's eyes could. Behind Josef's back she dared to wink at me.

CHAPTER
TWELVE

Nadia and I had no real chance to talk that evening. It would have been rude to our hosts to speak English. Ana knew very little, Josef none at all. Ana was complimentary about my scrappy Romanian, which was certainly improving. She did not want me to forget the Romanian half of me and poured out constant details about this old uncle's death and that new baby born to some distant cousin I had never heard of.

"Remember to tell your mother that," she insisted. "She is sure to be interested."

I promised. I could not possibly carry it all in my head, so I was driven to making stealthy notes. This immediately alarmed Josef. "He wants to know what you are writing in your little book," said Nadia, embarrassed. I explained tactfully. This only increased the alarm which now spread to all of them. "They ask you not to take out anything like this in writing," said Nadia. "Someone at the frontier might go through your papers — it would provide a nominal roll of the family, it might seem suspicious — "

"I've thought of that." I grinned as I held out the open notebook for them all to see. Nadia knitted her brows in complexity. "I do not understand. Who *is* this nineteenth-century German composer? I have never heard of him."

"You won't have. I've just invented him. It's so simple really."

She read on for a few lines, then her frown vanished and she burst out laughing. Ana quickly joined in. Josef did not look so amused, shocked rather.

"You have put back the dates a hundred years!" cried Ana.

"And changed the place-names to German or Austrian!" said Nadia. "So our little cousin Franz was born in Stuttgart in 1882 instead of Suceava in 1982 — " She turned to meet Josef's disapproving frown. "It's quite *safe*. Nothing more natural — Greg's a musician, of course he'd make notes like these. They'll jog his memory about all we've been telling him. Oh, for heaven's sake, Josef, what *harm* is it doing?"

"It is not true," said Josef stolidly.

"And we *all* in this country — *always* — speak the truth? Without fear?" Her scorn was venomous.

I tried to change the subject and restore peace. Unfortunately the conversation got round to the local news story of the Hungarian pastor and his broken windows, which provoked Josef to a torrent of propaganda. "The man is a trouble-maker," he declared. "If his windows are broken he has only himself to blame. We do not want his sort here."

It was a relief next morning to escape by ourselves again and talk freely.

Yesterday had shaken Nadia. "How wise your mother was, all those years ago! She saw what was coming. The Comrade had only just become leader – not that things were good under the Party, even before that – but ever since then they have got worse and worse. He is a megalomaniac. And that wife of his!"

"I can imagine." I remembered her face when they came round after our concert. Nadia had told me a malicious story going the rounds of Bucharest, illustrating Elena's lack of culture. She had been presented with a copy of the *Venus de Milo* and did not even know that the statue had been minus its arms since its first discovery. "Why do you bring me this rubbish?" she was said to have complained, and as no one dared to expose her ignorance a tame sculptor had to be hired to repair it.

Nadia could not swear that this story was true, "But it has brought a lot of laughs into our dull lives," she said.

The Ceausescu family similarly excited her contempt. "The fat cats! Planted in their cosy little jobs everywhere, brothers, sisters, sons, daughters. I wish I could get out of this country – as your mother did! But what hope is there?"

"Have you ever tried to get a passport?" I asked.

"I applied two years ago – to go with a youth party to Czechoslovakia – a safe Communist country then!" She made a face. "The same side of the Iron Curtain." Only within the last month had the Communists fallen there.

Two years ago, I thought, you'd only be sixteen. "Didn't they give it to you?"

She shrugged. "It was neither refused nor granted. It was delayed. Officials find it easier to do nothing. I asked again. I must 'wait my turn', it was 'going through the proper channels'. The date for the holiday went by. It was no use making any more fuss."

"You haven't applied again?"

"It might be unwise to stir things up. If they found that the first application had never been granted it would look suspicious. When they found that I was living in Bucharest without a permit it would look worse."

I saw her point.

She sighed, then pulled herself together. "See, we have almost reached the Green Forest. Look at the sunshine! We must not spoil this day."

We had bought a picnic lunch on our way, brioches and cheese-filled pastries, apples and a bottle of mineral water, for we could hardly expect the summertime huts and cafés to be open now. I had expected a forest of dark mysterious pinewoods, something out of Grimms' fairy tales. Not so. We walked through bright golden clearings over leaf-carpets of rustling brown and red. There were oaks and beeches, ivy and greyish creeper dangling in festoons.

We discussed our interests and ambitions. Sometimes I had to check my confident tongue. It was unfair to tantalize her with my freedom, when it was so hard to see similar opportunities beckoning to her. I could not imagine that Romania just now offered an alluring future – least of all for an independent girl like Nadia. Nor must I babble on about Britain or other countries I had seen. But she was so curious, so alert. She made me talk about them, she was a bird pouncing on crumbs.

"Oh, I have talked to many foreigners in the shop," she admitted, "until Madame began to scowl! But to talk with you like this is much nicer."

"I talk too much about myself –"

"Do not all boys?" she said with gentle wickedness. "But *you* are much more interesting. I think."

The sky grew pink between the bare branches. We made our way back to the town in the gloaming. We went round by the Hungarian church to see if the situation had changed. The crowd was larger than on the previous day. This was Saturday and the working week was over.

"There must be *thousands*," said Nadia.

They formed a thick cordon right round the block in which the church was located. Glum-faced militiamen stood about on the fringes. She identified several Securitate agents for me. They were all in plain clothes, trying to look inconspicuous, but their type was unmistakable.

The crowd talked freely. They seemed less inhibited than the people in Bucharest. They looked mostly ordinary Romanians – Hungarians were now quite a minority, and the psalm-singing churchgoers of yesterday were less dominant. Nadia got talking to a woman from the next block of flats. Had anything special been happening?

"What can, my dear? Too many of us!"

The pastor and his wife, she said, were safe indoors and no one could touch them. The mayor had been and begged the crowd to go home, but no one would budge. The police had made no move.

The woman laughed cynically. "They say they're only here to keep the peace. It's the bishop who wants to move the pastor out to Mineu. Nothing to do with them!" She snorted. "They say that to save their faces. If they could get to his door and break it down they'd have him out in no time. But they daren't." She looked round the crowd with a triumphant expression.

We went on home so that Nadia could help her sister with the evening meal. After we had eaten we gave Pavel a riotous play-hour. Then Josef settled down to a football match and looked sour at our rumpus, so Nadia scooped up the little boy for a hilarious bath and I helped Ana wash the dishes, which she seemed to regard as extraordinary but not unwelcome behaviour from a young man. I assured her that it was not uncommon in the decadent West.

As it was Saturday there was no need for anyone

to go to bed early. But Josef was glued to his television and did not encourage conversation. Ana had a heap of mending. It was she who encouraged us to go out again if we felt inclined. Perhaps we would like to go to a disco?

"That's a good idea," said Nadia brightly – rather too brightly, I fancied, and I proved right. It was the last thing she wanted to do. Like me, she was anxious to know if anything had developed outside the pastor's.

The boulevard lay straight and silvery under a moon that was just past the full, and riding high above the old citadel.

We found a crowd still milling restlessly around the block. Its composition had changed. Faithful parishioners were less in evidence. It was more like an ordinary Saturday evening crowd, drawn by the hope of a little excitement. The police were still there in force, watchful but passive. There was an argumentative element, young like ourselves.

Nadia spotted the woman who had been there before. She asked if anything had happened yet.

"Nay, not a thing. The pastor and his wife haven't come out – we thought they might have done. These lads have been hoping he'd make a speech, maybe. I reckon he'll not do anything so foolish. It would be playing into the hands of you-know-who. They'd have something on him then." She sniffed. "He did send out word – come to church as usual in the morning, he'll be there. But that's not good enough for some of these young tearaways, it's action they're after."

She eyed me with interest. "You and your friend don't want to get mixed up in anything." She wished us good night and made off.

"Getting mixed up" was exactly what Nadia and I were after. We were becoming infected by the mounting tension, the exhilarating scent of revolt. Perhaps people had taken as much of the dictatorship as they could stand.

Voluble groups were disputing keenly, turning occasionally to taunt the police. An older man sought to restrain them. "You'll do the pastor no good," he pleaded. "If there's any disorder, he'll get the blame." I doubt if some of his listeners cared much. The pastor's disagreement with his bishop did not concern them. What they wanted was a pretext for a demonstration against the government. If the pastor would not lead it they would stir things up themselves.

A police inspector told them to disperse. "What do you *want*?" he asked wearily – and incautiously gave them just the cue they needed.

A measured, repetitive chant began. "What do we want? Bread! What do we want? Bread!" Then another group started a different slogan. "Down – with – the ration cards!"

Fresh faces appeared at windows all around. The crowd began to simmer, then bubble like a saucepan coming to the boil. A voice yelled. "Why waste time here? If you want a meeting, let's go up the town!"

Obviously the pastor was not coming out. A movement started. The crowd began to uncoil itself into a column, flowing across the boulevard, over the bridge, into the moonlit park. We followed with the rest. People were tearing down posters and portraits of the Comrade, hurling them derisively into the black water. They were singing now, the same song apparently they had sung at this spot two years before, "Awake, Romania!" I murmured to Nadia, "Romania won't have much chance to sleep tonight."

As we marched up the hill we heard the splintering of shop windows in the old town ahead of us. Oh, no, I thought, disappointed, not *looting* — surely? I had hoped for some idealistic demonstration in the name of Liberty. We had enough mindless vandalism in the West. It would be a shame if support for the pastor turned into something as squalid as that. It sounded that way, though — the crash of plate glass, the breaking of hinge and shutter, the exultant yell that signalled entry. It might, of course, be a foodshop. Under present conditions there might be justification...

When we reached the scene of the uproar it proved to be only a dull-looking bookshop we had passed the previous day. Not many people want books so badly that they break in to loot them, but I saw guys running up the street with armfuls.

I bumped into one girl who looked like a student. She was hugging a stack of books high as her chin. One fell and bumped at my feet. Instinctively I stooped to pick it up for her but she did not bother to grab it back, just went clicking her way up the hill on her high heels. The books looked identical – the bright moonlight showed the title bold as day: *The Method of Constructing the Multi-Laterally Developed Socialist Society*. It did not sound the sort of book people would smash windows to steal. It proved to be one of about thirty uniform volumes of somebody's collected works. You can guess whose. I read the name in thick letters, *N Ceausescu*.

It was the Party bookshop they were wrecking. From just up the hill, where the street turned into Opera Square, there was a sudden hiss, a blinding flash of light, then pungent clouds of billowing smoke.

Someone had got hold of a can of petrol. Flames were leaping skywards from a mound of books by the fountain in the middle of the square. Silhouetted figures were capering round in a war-dance, feeding the fire. More than one portrait of the Comrade was curling and shrivelling in the heat.

Nadia laughed up in my face, her teeth flickering in the rosy light. "We should have brought Josef's!" she cried. She looked a proper devil in that setting.

We were both carried away by the excitement round us. The police had melted away; no one was lifting a finger. It was as though Romania had indeed awakened and the iron dictatorship had collapsed like a house of cards. Or the walls of Jericho at the blast of Joshua's trumpets. It seemed too good to be true.

The crowd had pushed on to batter at some other door. "It's the local Party Headquarters," whispered Nadia between awe and glee. People were running back to the fire with bundles of files and pamphlets, more posters, more portraits.

One gaunt youth was stooping over a flag he had spread flat across the paving stones. He had found a big pair of office scissors and was struggling to cut a somewhat ragged hole in the centre of the cloth. The flag was the national tricolour of blue, yellow and red, and it was the Communist addition to the centre that he was determined to remove. He leapt to his feet suddenly with an almost blood-curdling howl of triumph, raised the flag on its pole, and brandished it against the sky. The moon shone through the tattered hole he had managed to cut. Looking up, we saw for the first time what was to become the rallying symbol for the next mad days.

As though at a signal everyone began to sing.

CHAPTER THIRTEEN

You could not expect that midnight mood of elation to survive into the cold light of a December morning.

Especially as it was a Sunday morning. Neither Josef nor Ana had to go to work. And whatever their private beliefs might have been Josef was too timid to allow for any church-going in that atheistic state. It would have drawn attention to him, made the authorities wonder if he was a sound Party man.

So it was goodbye to the cosy little breakfasts that Nadia and I had enjoyed on previous days. It was a family meal. The atmosphere was relieved only by the antics of little Pavel, who was too young to know anything about politics.

Josef and Ana had heard the distant shouting last night, seen the column of shadowy figures marching across the park to the old city. Ana had been worried lest we got mixed up in the trouble, and were hurt or even arrested. Josef, I imagine, had been worried lest we got mixed up in it, full stop.

Our own welfare was of little concern to him. His young sister-in-law was a problem he would have been glad to dispense with. Her uninvited guest from abroad was another, even more so. Though I don't think he would have been pleased to hear that I'd been picked up by the police and thrown into a cell. That would have raised awkward questions, like who are you staying with? Which was the very last thing poor old Josef wanted.

He said now, making a grotesque effort to sound friendly, "Let me see, Gregory, when do you have to leave us?"

"Day after tomorrow. I've worked out a route to take in Belgrade."

"So soon?" said Ana. She at least sounded genuinely sorry. She seemed to like me all right. Or maybe it was just that she was pleased to see Nadia so full of the joy of life.

I, too, felt genuinely sorry. I'd have liked Romania to have gone on a little longer. Things were beginning to get really interesting. I wondered how they would develop after the next few days. If it had been anywhere else I could have depended on Nadia to send me long letters and tell me everything. But as things stood here I doubted whether she'd be able to write to me at all, and certainly any account of an event like last night would be struck out by the censor.

We must crack this problem somehow. We

must talk it over in the next two days, try to fix some system for keeping in touch. I was really determined on that.

When we'd done our share of the tidying up after breakfast we offered to take Pavel with us for an airing in the sunshine. Ana accepted the offer gratefully, Josef less so, but he may have felt that having the boy would cramp our style and lessen the risk of our behaving unsuitably.

"Be good," Ana instructed. And smiling at us over Pavel's head she murmured, "That goes for all of you." Nadia had managed to give her a whispered account, in the kitchen, of the demonstration last night and the bonfire in Opera Square.

"When am I anything but good?" Nadia demanded.

"I could give examples."

Once we were out on the boulevard we both turned instinctively the same way. We must check on the situation at the pastor's. Pavel protested loudly. He wanted to walk along the embankment and look down at the ducks.

"Later," said Nadia.

"Now!"

"Greg and I want to go this way first."

"No!"

"Yes."

"Why?"

"It is a two-to-one vote against you. Democracy!"

"What's democracy?"

"Something that one day you may have to learn about."

"At school?" he asked hopefully.

"I doubt that — under the Comrade. You had better begin learning now."

After the turmoil of last night the boulevard stretched ahead of us with the boring emptiness of a December Sunday morning.

A street-sweeper was clearing up some torn strips of poster, empty beer bottles, a lost glove. But nothing special had happened round here.

We drew closer to the Hungarian Church. Now we saw occasional clusters of people talking excitedly. Respectable churchgoers, most of them looked like. But not walking devoutly to morning service. Coming away, more likely, with disappointment and alarm written on their faces. Nadia accosted one old lady.

"Is the service over already?"

The woman looked at her. "The service has never begun! There is a notice on the door — just a scribble — the services are cancelled until further notice."

"What has happened to the pastor?"

"God knows, my dear. They came for him at three o'clock in the morning. They broke down his door — he wasn't there. So they went upstairs to the church. They found him inside, with his pyjamas on under his cassock, holding a bible, kneeling with his poor wife at the altar."

Nadia gave a little gasp of horror. She looked at me, and I nodded to show that I understood what the old woman was saying. Pavel gaped.

120

"The policemen beat him – shamefully. Then they took him downstairs and threw him into one of their cars. And drove off. All the neighbours were awake by then. They saw it all."

"What about his wife?"

"They took her off as well," said the old woman. "I don't know where."

What a country! And last night everyone had been singing and dancing in the street, kidding themselves that by sheer weight of numbers they could defy the government. The police just bided their time, waiting for us all to go home to bed. Easy.

I was suddenly aware that a policeman, a man in uniform, with a neat moustache, was eyeing me with more interest than I cared for. "Perhaps," I murmured gently to Nadia, "we should be keeping our promise to Pavel."

But as Nadia said a final word to the old woman, and turned away, the man came walking over with that slow deliberate pace that police the world over seem to develop. Perhaps it gives them more time to think, before committing themselves to speech.

His question surprised me. "Hungarian?" he said sharply.

"No. British."

It seemed to be his turn to look surprised. "You have a British passport?"

"Yes."

He examined it as though he had never seen such a document. "You are not a journalist?" His tone was wary. Then he relaxed slightly as he saw my date of birth and my description as student, which is the same in Romanian.

It was often a tricky business, calling for a split-second decision, whether to show that I understood the language or to act dumb. In this case it seemed better to be truthful.

Nadia seemed to think the same. "He is my cousin from England," she said. "He has been staying in Bucharest – he is leaving for Austria the day after tomorrow."

The policeman relaxed noticeably. I realized afterwards he was anxious lest I was a Hungarian and might go straight back across the frontier blabbing about what had been done to the Hungarian church here. He was less worried about my turning out to be British – so long as it did not mean I was a journalist. He would hardly expect to meet one in Timisoara, and if I had been it would have set the alarm bells ringing.

Pavel saved the situation by butting in at that moment with a vehement demand to be taken to see the ducks. The policeman relaxed completely. He was not one of the Securitate, just an ordinary local cop. He bent down and patted Pavel's cheek, asked his age as if he were really interested. He straightened up and smiled at us, at Nadia especially. He must have decided that I was not a suspicious character after all, though I wore foreign clothes and was near the scene of last night's agitation.

So we got to the park and sauntered along the embankment, talking in low voices, while the child threw fragments of breakfast roll to the delighted ducks. In Josef's home there was no great shortage of bread, no need to go out and chant slogans about it at public demonstrations.

"This is terrible," said Nadia.

The news of the pastor's forcible removal was certainly a cruel disappointment after the crowd's unopposed celebrations last night. What had happened to the pastor – and his wife? We were desperate to know.

"Some people listen to Budapest," said Nadia. "And other foreign stations."

"I bet Josef doesn't," I said pessimistically.

She nodded. "I'll tell you who does, though. Uncle Sandor. With the radio turned down. Living alone. There's no one to tell tales of him. Of course, the news may not have got out yet. But Uncle Sandor may have heard something locally. If they've put the pastor in the cells they can't hide that for long. It'll soon get round the town."

We agreed that if anyone had information it would most likely to be the old violinist. We had to take Pavel home now for the midday meal. Afterwards we could easily find an excuse to come out again, and we'd make straight for Uncle Sandor's.

"We can say we want some real exercise," said Nadia. "You can't walk fast with a little boy, when he's stopping every few yards to talk to the ducks."

Josef raised no objection when the time came. "Of course," he said. "Gregory must see as much

123

as possible of our beautiful town. All the latest improvements. His time is all too short."

Not short enough for you, I thought.

Soon we were crossing the river again and striking briskly across the park. The old city rose before us in the soft golden light of the afternoon.

All signs of last night's disorder had been cleared away: the windows of the bookshop were boarded over; in the square the ashes of the bonfire had been swept up, the blackened circle hosed down.

The streets were quiet at this hour, but somehow I felt a tension in the air. Parties of young people mooched aimlessly about or stood talking at corners. There were more policemen than usual, mostly in pairs. Some moved along the narrow street, checking shop doors for damage, sometimes lurking in the shadowy entrances. At sight of them the youths became instantly alert, staring back furtively, or moving off as though on a common impulse, like birds taking flight.

Once we heard distant sounds, crashes and exultant shouting. Then the moaning of a police car down some street in front of us. We looked at each other. More looting? Or a political demonstration? The policemen we passed looked uneasy. Some were armed. They fingered their weapons.

We were not, ourselves, looking for trouble. Only information. Uncle Sandor's was the best place to make for.

"He knows everybody, everything that goes

on," said Nadia. "If anything has happened, he knows. And probably if anything is going to happen. He has so many friends."

Somehow I could believe that.

When he opened the door to us Nadia said, "I hope we are not interrupting your afternoon nap?"

"Who can sleep at a time like this?" He led us in. We told him all that we knew, but he had already been telephoned by a friend. As we had hoped, he knew more than we did.

"No, he is not under arrest. They beat him up, yes. That is routine with the Securitate." His lip curled. "Otherwise, they are playing this as coolly as they can. They do not want publicity. They have simply taken him to Mineu – which, after all, is where his gutless bishop had ordered him." Uncle Sandor felt free to speak disrespectfully of the bishop. He was not Uncle Sandor's bishop, indeed (in his eyes) not a proper bishop at all.

"Is his wife there?" asked Nadia.

"Oh, yes. As I say, he is not under arrest. Though there are police there to make sure he does not try to come back. It's not far away, of course. But very isolated. He's cut off from his supporters. Though, of course –" Uncle Sandor's smile was a little crafty – "he'll manage to get messages in and out somehow. He's tough, Lazlo. They won't break him down easily."

"Break him down?" I echoed.

"They'll try to make him see reason. Realize that he can't go on with all this outspoken criticizing of the government. They'll try to soften him up with promises. If he'll go on television and take back all he's been saying, there'll be no trouble. They're jumpy — especially after yesterday evening. They don't *want* trouble."

It struck me that the old man seemed remarkably well informed. We did not ask him how he knew all this. I guessed that if he was not one of those who were managing to get messages through to the pastor he must be in close touch with somebody who was. You don't ask too closely. Sometimes it is better not to know too much — or at least not to show that you do.

Uncle Sandor consulted his watch and began to twiddle with his radio. Suddenly an announcer's voice swelled up in mid-sentence. Uncle Sandor hastily turned down the volume. I could make nothing of the language. I guessed it was Hungarian, transmitted from Budapest, which was really quite close. Uncle Sandor seemed to understand what the man was saying. Nadia, with knitted brows, was straining to puzzle out a word or two here and there. After a few minutes they exclaimed in unison and became doubly intent. Even I caught the pastor's name, the hated word "Securitate", and then the name of the hamlet to which he had been removed. My friends exchanged glances of triumph.

"The news is out!" cried the old man. 'Budapest has it. Other countries will pick it up from there. Excellent." He got up, went to a cupboard, and produced glasses and a bottle of *tuica*. We sipped it, and drank the health of the pastor and his family. We

126

talked on, reviewing all the possibilities of the situation.

After about an hour the telephone rang. Uncle Sandor apologized to us in his old-world way. The conversation was brief and conducted in very discreet terms, not because of our presence, I was sure, but for fear of other, unknown listeners.

"'*Not* responding to treatment', you say? Ah, I see what you mean... Oh, that is good. So he will not get too bored during his convalescence... That is very helpful... Everyone will be *most* concerned for his recovery... Yes. By all means. Goodbye."

He came back to his seat. Nadia looked at him eagerly. She had no need to ask.

"That is what I wanted to hear," he said. "They have smuggled a radio into his room – the police are not with him all the time. They watch the house, of course, they come in at intervals to continue their persuasions – pressing him to appear on television."

"But he isn't weakening? He's not 'responding to treatment'?"

"Not he! I can't imagine Lazlo."

Nor could I. I remembered the hefty young man I had met, patiently boarding up his windows against all comers.

"But it will be a great help to him – and Edit," Uncle Sandor continued, "if they can tune in to foreign radio and know that they are not forgotten, not alone. Somehow we must keep the publicity going." His brow furrowed as he thought hard. "I have an old friend myself who works for a news agency in Budapest. I will ring his office tomorrow. We must all do anything we can."

We must all do anything we can...

The words struck home. That meant me, even me. What could *I* do? A foreigner... Ah, wasn't that just it? A foreigner...

My father had friends who were journalists. If I telephoned him, perhaps he could pass on to them what I knew, and somehow, somewhere, a useful paragraph could be slipped into a national newspaper. How could I communicate to him the sense of urgency I felt? I considered the scanty facts. It would not seem exactly headline stuff. I could see the tolerant smiles at the golf club when he told them of his call from his son, all excited by this local rumpus in Transylvania or some such place.

Suddenly came a flash of inspiration. I needed a contact who would really care about the pastor's ill-treatment. And someone who would be in a position to do something.

Holy Joe's uncle! The Methodist bishop – but a very different sort of bishop from the one here, who was timidly doing the government's work.

Joe would have told his uncle what had happened to all those bibles that the American churches had sent out to Romania, posted him those recycled pages on which the faint imprint of the Holy Writ could still be deciphered. Joe's uncle was a formidable character. If he got this further news from Romania I could see him reaching for the phone.

First, though, I would have to reach for the phone myself. I must try to get through to Joe today, in England.

A public phone would be safest, as in Bucharest. I obviously could not make the call from Josef's. It would be unfair to involve Uncle Sandor. I felt he was taking risks enough and I did not want to add to them. I'd do it from one of the hotels we had passed.

Just then Uncle Sandor's phone rang. He answered it with the same discretion as before.

It was a short conversation. Hurried and urgent. He hung up, looking grave.

"A young friend of mine..." he said. "She works at the airport. The plane has just come in from Bucharest. With some very important passengers. Coman..."

Nadia drew in her breath sharply.

For my benefit Uncle Sandor explained, "General Coman, that is. Central Committee for Military and Security Affairs. And several others she thought were generals. In Timisoara! It sounds ominous. Even allowing for last night's revolt! I suppose the Comrade is furious because it wasn't crushed immediately. He'd have liked arrests, one or two boys shot down perhaps. But to send men like Coman!" The old musician looked really worried. "A sledgehammer to crack a nut. That would be quite like the Comrade. But – *several* sledgehammers?"

I took the opportunity to tell them of my idea to telephone Joe. They liked it.

It was time to be going anyhow. First, though –

"Just a moment," I said, and tore a sheet from my notebook, and scribbled down just what I wanted to say.

We said goodbye and went out into the gloom. There seemed to be a lot of noise going on in the distance. Singing and shouting. What sounded like anti-Ceausescu slogans. Darkness lends courage to a crowd. People were coming out on the streets again, determined to make another night of it.

"This is exciting," said Nadia. "I hope you can get through to your Holy Joe. It will be good to feel that we have done something."

"However small," I said realistically.

"One never knows. It is all we *can do*."

The hotel was obliging. There was a stinging service-charge for an international call and I knew I had better tip generously. They seemed glad to see us. We got through quite quickly and to my relief it was the living Joe at the other end.

"Greg? Hi! Where are—"

I cut him short. "Listen," I said, "*I'm* OK, but I've got an important message for your uncle."

"My uncle?"

"The bishop. Write it down, will you? Carefully."

"Sure!"

I read my note at dictation speed, spelling out "Timisoara". I heard Joe exclaim softly as he caught on to the significance of the message. I got as far as the generals' arrival from Bucharest. Instantly there was a click and the line went dead.

130

Nadia, squeezed beside me in the booth, heard and said quickly, "We'd better go."

"I hadn't finished. We've been cut off. Let me try—"

"No. Quick. We go." She dragged me out.

I went to pay for the call. The man at the desk gave me an odd look. "It happens all the time, sir. If you will wait I can perhaps get you reconnected."

"No," whispered Nadia urgently. "We go."

He seemed reluctant to let us. "If you will sit down, sir, I am sure..."

Nadia's grip on my arm was insistent. I dropped the money on the counter and we rushed out into the darkness.

"That man will know me again," I said lightly.

"He knows he may have to describe you. Have you still got that bit of paper?"

"Yes."

She snatched it from me, tore it across, and dropped the pieces through a grating.

I saw the point. At a time like this we might easily be stopped and questioned by some zealous policeman. It would not do to have that bit of paper in my pocket.

The night grew noisy. Ahead of us there seemed to be a public meeting going on in Opera Square. The crowd was singing. It sounded like nothing so much as the singing I'd heard when watching some great international football match on television. It was in fact a football-supporters' song that they were singing. I found that out later. It had been taken up by the Polish Solidarity movement when they were protesting against their Communist government, and then, during this year of unrest and rebellion, it had spread through one country after another in Eastern Europe, each country fitting its own words.

That night I heard it for the first time. In Romanian.

I heard something else too, a deafening sound overhead.

"What's that?" cried Nadia.

"Sounds like a chopper!" I had almost to bellow in her ear.

I looked up. It was indeed a helicopter, like a giant black insect hovering low over the gabled roofs, its rotor blades spinning. Then suddenly the shadow blotting out the stars was gone, even the stars were gone, as the great eye of the searchlight opened and caught us in its dazzling whiteness. It tracked along the street, picking out the throng of figures – men, women, even quite small children – hurrying along in the same direction, to see what was going on in Opera Square. A rare Sunday evening excitement for this small provincial city.

More excitement, indeed, than anyone had bargained for.

The helicopter had moved on. One could hear oneself speak again. One could hear the voices and footsteps all around, the swelling chorus of the Solidarity song in front. And suddenly another new sound – a series of pop-pop explosions, as if someone was letting off fireworks.

The crowd ahead of us was turning back with screams and panic-stricken cries. Coughing and spluttering, they came charging down the street like a buffalo stampede. I grabbed Nadia. We flattened ourselves into a doorway. And the fumes of the tear-gas took us by the throat.

CHAPTER FOURTEEN

I had seen it all before, a dozen times. On television.

The flying figures, staggering, falling, racing on... The policemen in pursuit, with their flailing batons and their riot shields... in countless cities round the world.

But this was different. We were in it. We could not switch off or turn to another channel.

I clapped my handkerchief over my streaming eyes. Nadia uttered something between a cough and a cry, muffled by the headscarf she had pulled over her face. We could only stay there, shrinking back into the doorway. The patter and scuttle of ordinary footsteps gave place to the thunder of heavy boots as the militiamen pelted past. Some wretch had fallen; they stopped to rain blows on him, cursing savagely. The fumes by now were thinning. It became possible to speak again, to see mistily.

Nadia groped for my hand. "If we can get past the square – " she gasped. She drew me round the corner into another street. I followed her guidance. She knew this town, I did not. All that mattered was to reach her home.

They were singing again in the square. And as we turned into another, wider, thoroughfare, we were caught up in a throng that was marching purposefully forward, chanting anti-Ceausescu slogans in unison, holding up home-made banners denouncing the government, demanding liberty for Pastor Tokes. Others waved Romanian flags, but now every flag you saw had its heart torn out – there was a ragged hole in the centre where the republican emblem had been.

It was good to be in a high-spirited crowd again, confident and defiant, unafraid. I suppose we all lent courage to each other. The singing of the greater multitude in the square ahead of us was like a beacon of victory, guiding us forward to join them.

Then abruptly the head of the column halted. We crowded up behind until we were so close that we could not move another step forward. A row of helmets barred the street from wall to wall. At the back of them some bulky vehicle loomed.

A loud hailer ordered us to disperse. We yelled defiance. Missiles began to fly. At such times someone always finds things to throw.

I braced myself for more tear-gas. This time we should be in the thick of it. I must not get parted from Nadia. If things got really ugly I must get her out of here.

It was not tear-gas this time. The vehicle proved to be a water cannon. A few moments later they let us have it – a great jet of water under high pressure, cutting a swathe through the column, sending us toppling and reeling like ninepins.

I felt as if I'd been kicked by a horse. I went over backwards, winded, incapable of action or speech. Nadia sprawled in the road beside me, but she had missed the full force, for I felt her hand cupping my head, heard her voice in my ear. "Greg! Are you all right?"

She ducked as the jet of water swung to and fro over us. People were scrambling to their feet, only to be bowled over again on the wet cobbles.

I gasped, "Got to get out of here!" When the jet ceased the police would charge. We did not want cracked heads or broken collar-bones when those clubs came raining down. You may want to be a hero, you may think you are ready to face anything, but you can't – literally can't – face a water cannon that's aimed at you. You end up flat on your back.

We went with all the other fugitives until the militiamen broke ranks and came after us with a blood-curdling howl. If the authorities had been too timid to act yesterday they were certainly getting their nerve back now. No doubt those generals who'd just flown in from Bucharest were bracing them up.

For the moment this particular section of the

crowd was dispersed. But we could hear the great swell of voices singing in the square, and then, like hammer blows of thunderous sound, the measured slogans of defiance.

The numbers crammed into Opera Square must be tremendous. A town like Timisoara would hardly have the force to cope with it. Tear-gas and water cannon, yes — irresistible at the point where they were operating. But they could not be everywhere at once. And as they broke up the crowd in one street people slipped round corners and reformed somewhere else.

We did not join another marching column. "This way, Greg!" Nadia led me round another corner, and suddenly we were in the square on the fringe of the multitude which almost filled it. Our soaked jeans clung to our legs. I was bleakly conscious that this was mid-December. Perhaps there was a chance now to slip unobtrusively round the back of the demonstration, and then it should be easy to get home across the open park.

Nadia had other views. Her blood was up. She was unconscious of the cold and wet. For the first time we almost quarrelled.

Over the heads of the demonstrators I could see grey shapes edging along one side of the square. Some were armoured personnel carriers, others were tanks, their guns pivoting, slanting down into the horizontal position so that they could fire at point-blank range. It was an ugly sight.

"Come on," I said desperately, "we'd better get out of here."

"We must do something!"

"What *can* we do?" The people in front were still singing and shouting crazily. Their home-made banners swayed like sails on an angry sea. I took her arm for emphasis. "They've got tanks. We can't achieve anything."

She shook her hand off, furiously. "Of course, this is not your country! But it is mine."

Her words were like a slap in the face. And for an instant I felt I could have slapped hers, literally.

Then the shooting started. The automatic chatter of the Kalashnikov rifles. And it wasn't over our heads. The screaming was not just the screaming of hysterical fright. There were cries of pain. People were falling down or staggering back, bent, hobbling, clutching at friends for support. It was chaos. Mercilessly the firing rattled on.

Nadia stooped and picked up a flag that someone had dropped. She held it up defiantly and started forward. Did she imagine she was Joan of Arc or something? It was suicidal.

"You little idiot!" I plunged after her, cursing. Another thing I could never have imagined myself doing. Then, horrors, down she went.

It took me only about two seconds to reach her, but in that brief space a lot rushed through my mind, and it was not pleasant.

Thank God, she did not seem to be hurt. She had simply dropped down on her knees and was frantically trying to help some woman sprawled on the ground.

She looked round. "Oh, Greg!" she gasped.

"She's hurt – but she thinks she can stand if we help her – "

It was simple enough, now I was there to lend a hand. The woman cried out in pain when I touched her arm, but she managed to stay on her feet.

At least we had found something we *could* do, I have only confused memories of what else was happening around us.

The firing slackened, the shouting and chanting died away, the square was emptying fast. There were other little clusters like ourselves, moving slowly because we were helping the casualties. A few were limping away unaided. And, glancing back, I saw that there were other people on the ground, not moving at all. And now an advancing line of helmeted figures, their rifles at the ready, peering down at the bodies, prodding them with their feet. In the distance a little boy was crying piteously, inconsolably, until someone took him away.

We followed the general drift of the wounded into the shelter of the public gardens. The woman protested that she was all right, and as we stood there, dithering uncertainly, some of her friends appeared and relieved us of further responsibility. There was no reason then why we should not make our way home.

"I am soaked," said Nadia in a small voice. "What about you?"

"OK. But I shan't be sorry to get into something dry." I think neither of us felt like walking faster. The life had gone out of us. My feet felt like lead.

"I've lost my flag," she said, with a mixture of humour and pathos.

"You must have dropped it when you went to help that woman. Never mind," I said gently. "You wanted to do something. What you did do was the most sensible thing you could."

"I hope she'll be all right. Oh, Greg, wasn't it *awful*?"

Ana opened the door to us. "Thank God you're back! We heard firing – I was so worried!" Then, as we stepped into the lighted hallway, she let out a scream. "*Nadia!*"

I followed her horrified stare and, as I saw the dark red blotch on Nadia's sweater, my own heart seemed to stop.

"I'm all right," said Nadia. "It's someone else's blood."

CHAPTER
FIFTEEN

The voices brought Pavel running, luckily too late to catch those last words. Wide-eyed, delighted, he cried out in a shrill parody of adult disapproval:

"Auntie Nadia! You *have* made a mess of yourself!"

"Shut up!" she told him, with unusual tartness.

"Run away, dear," said Ana desperately. "We're busy." She put an arm round her sister and ushered her into the bathroom.

Pavel turned to me. "Were the fireworks good?"

"Fireworks? Oh – yes..." I began feebly.

Josef stood in the living-room doorway, smoke curling from the cigarette between his fingers. "We were explaining the noise in the distance."

"Someone will have a whole heap of explaining to do!" The strength came back into my voice.

"I take it – " Josef gave a warning glance down at his son. He chose his words carefully, the meaning well wrapped up. "I take it that the authorities found it necessary to use firm measures – to restore law and order?"

"You could say that." I added contemptuously, "I am sure *they* will."

He turned back into the living-room and I followed him. I was impatient to strip off my clammy jeans but with the girls in the bathroom, privacy was hard to find.

Josef had clearly disliked my tone. He said with weighty disapproval, "My wife has been frantic with anxiety. It is not good for her in her present condition. It was irresponsible of you to let Nadia—"

"Does anyone 'let' Nadia? She's not a child, she's a young woman, she can think for herself."

"She is undisciplined. But you, of course, coming from the West, do not believe in discipline." He sneered. He did not like anything much that came from the West – except its cigarettes. But his anxious curiosity overcame him. With another meaning glance at Pavel, now playing on the floor with a miniature car, he said, "This nation needs discipline. That is why our government must sometimes use a firm hand. A few shots over the heads of a mob may occasionally be unavoidable."

"A lot of people found these shots difficult to avoid. You saw for yourself. The blood on Nadia's sweater—"

"Sh!"

I ignored his warning. "A lot of people were hit. The soldiers were *not* firing over our heads. It was outrageous – almost a massacre."

His hands fluttered in agitation. "We had better wait – there will be a statement in the news bulletin, no doubt. We must not exaggerate. Or we shall be doing the enemy's work for him."

"The enemy?"

"Foreigners seize on rumours and distort them to harm our government. At a moment like this a good citizen must be doubly careful. A few careless words can do great harm."

And *you* will be doubly careful, I told myself. You're dead scared already, having me as a guest under your roof. I heard the sisters move across into Nadia's room. I seized some dry clothes, and escaped to the bathroom. When I came back Ana was starting to lay the table for the evening meal. There were no unusual noises coming from the old town. Normality seemed to be restored. An ordinary quiet Sunday night.

There was no mention of Timisoara in the news bulletin we watched. I was not surprised. What would have been hot news at home, huge headline stuff, could be held back and kept under wraps in a country like this, if the government wanted it that way.

Nadia and I could only speculate in whispers. There could be no stirring out again that night to find out what was happening. We owed that much consideration to Ana and we did not want an open row with Josef. Nadia tried to call Uncle Sandor, to assure him that we had got home safely and to ask him if he was all right. There was no answer. "We'll go and check on him in the morning," said Nadia.

It was good – it always was – to have the flat to ourselves when we met at breakfast the next day. Day was just breaking. We looked down on the boulevard. Thousands of people hurrying to work as usual. The trams and buses running. It was hard to believe that last night had really happened, that we had fled down that grey, frosty slope to get away from the bullets flying in Opera Square.

But it had been real. The nightmare had not been a dream. We switched on the radio, but there was still – incredibly – no word of any event in Timisoara. Perhaps it could be hushed up in the country as a whole? The Comrade after all had complete control of the media. Even he, though, could hardly obliterate the memory of the local people who had seen the horror for themselves.

Tomorrow would be our last breakfast together. Then it would be the train, the Yugoslav frontier, Belgrade.

"I hate leaving you at a time like this," I said.

"But you must. You cannot disappoint your parents."

Or Josef, I though grimly. If anyone was counting the days he was. He could not wait to get rid of this unwanted guest.

"After last night," I said, "I shall worry about you."

"That is... nice. But really you must not. As my dear brother-in-law assures us – " she made a face – "order has been restored in Timisoara. I'm not a complete fool, Greg. I wouldn't try to stop a tank with my bare hands."

Now we knew of each other's existence we were determined not to lose touch. She at least could have my home number and phone me safely from a public call box. But I followed the advice printed in my guidebook, *When leaving Romania never carry out the addresses of Romanian friends – memorize them instead. Discovery could mean an unpleasant interrogation for you.*

We set out for Uncle Sandor's. Crossing the park we found the workman sweeping the paths with more than usual care. One stretch they were spreading liberally with sand.

"There was blood there," Nadia whispered. A red-spattered rag dangled from a bush. One of the men snatched it down and thrust it into the pile of rubbish he was collecting.

There had been armoured personnel carriers ranged along the embankment. When we reached Opera Square there was a row of tanks. More sand, more aproned men with brooms, clean new grooves scored white by bullets across the face of buildings. But all was quiet now and the pigeons were stalking round the fountain in the middle.

Over in one corner was a blaze of colour which at first I took for a flower seller's stall. Then as we drew nearer I saw that a diminutive old lady in black was kneeling in front of it.

She was fastidiously dressed in hat and gloves, her handbag laid beside her on the flagstones. She was lighting a candle and carefully placing it amid a cluster of others, their wavering flames almost invisible in the pale sunshine.

A big man in uniform, with the blue cap-band of the Securitate, marched over to her and said something. She looked up. Her haggard face was like carved ivory. They argued quietly. Then he took her arm and helped her unwillingly to her feet, thrusting her gloves and bag into her hands.

"Murderers!" she said in a low tone, but with such distinct enunciation that the one word was like a whiplash in the silent square. She turned away and walked towards us. The Securitate man stepped into the midst of the flowers and candles, swinging his booted feet to left and right. Then he beckoned to a scared-looking street-cleaner to sweep everything away.

The old lady did not look back, but as she reached us she saw the outraged look on Nadia's face and paused. "I *think* that was the spot where my grandson was killed last night," she said. "This morning nobody will tell me anything. They have 'forgotten'. But *I* shall not forget. And neither will God."

The centre of the town was strangely quiet. People had gone to work, presumably because they dared not do otherwise. Big shops were open and as usual there were queues of hopeful customers. But some of the little shops remained shuttered, with crudely printed notices: *Closed till*

*further notice — for Family Reasons. Closed out
of Respect. Regret Closed Today: all enquiries
next door.*

One could read between the lines.

People exchanged greetings in subdued voices,
glancing over their shoulders, falling silent if
anyone in uniform went by. There were a lot
of uniforms about: the ordinary police, armed
border guards from some distance away, tank
crews and other regular troops. There were the
inevitable Securitate, some in uniform, others in
plain clothes. Nadia pointed out their Dacia cars,
which seemed to make up most of the traffic in
Timisoara that morning.

We were relieved to find Uncle Sandor safe in
his flat, crouched in front of his television set
with a transistor radio on one side and a tea
tray on the other.

"You got home safely?" he said. "Thank God
for that!"

He nodded constantly as we recounted the
details. It was evident that he was not hearing
them for the first time and was merely checking
up on accounts from other sources. He was like a
benevolent old spider, sitting at the centre of a web
and collecting information from his extraordinary
range of friends.

"The Comrade is mistaken if he imagines that
this business can be kept from the world outside.
Radio Budapest has the story already. They speak
of one thousand dead in Timisoara."

We both gasped, appalled. But he waved his
hands impatiently.

"It is an exaggeration. I am sure. God knows, it must have been bad enough. But a thousand! No, it is far too many."

We had no means of knowing. We had such fragmentary impressions of last night's horror. We had seen wounded people, we had seen motionless bodies in the square and suspected that some of them would never get up again.

"Journalists can guess." Uncle Sandor chuckled grimly. "And if the Comrade will not let them see for themselves, guess they will. Raising the figures all the time, as newspapers do."

"But," I said without thinking, "he can gag the newspapers!"

"In Romania, yes – but not abroad. And if he will not let the foreign journalists come in and report the facts as they are, he cannot complain if he forces them to guess."

We saw the results of that as we sat there throughout the morning, listening to the chatter of newsreaders on one station after another as Uncle Sandor turned the knob. At first they came from transmitters just beyond the frontier – Hungarian, Bulgarian, Yugoslav. Uncle Sandor had an incredible flair for languages and seemed able to grasp the drift of them all. "I am a Central European," he said drily. "You can live and die in one town – wars and revolutions wash over you and change your nationality. But not your heart." Some of the bulletins were given in Romanian and with Nadia's help I could follow them. Eventually we picked up English from the BBC.

The old violinist was right in his prediction of the ever-mounting casualty estimates. In the course of the morning the death-roll went up to five thousand. A Yugoslav news agency produced the top guess of sixty thousand.

It was all, of course, absurd. But even in Timisoara itself – though we could see the impossibility of the more alarming reports – no one could get a clear idea of the facts. Several friends telephoned Uncle Sandor while we were there, once a neighbour in the same building tapped at his door and there was a long, confidential whispering. But the truth was like some baffling jigsaw into which he could fit only such few pieces as reached him.

One of the phone calls was from a doctor friend. When Sandor hung up he turned to us. "There are dozens of wounded, he says, in his casualty ward. Mostly with gunshot wounds. We have several hospitals in Timisoara. His guess is that something like two hundred cases have been admitted."

"Two hundred!" exclaimed Nadia. It was better than the staggering figures of the foreign radio bulletins, but all the same – two hundred!

"There would be many others," said Sandor. "Some because the injuries were lighter and could be treated at home. Others, I'm afraid, because the person knew he was already on the files of the Securitate and did not want to draw attention to himself. Such people might go privately to a doctor they could trust. In other cases they may pay for it with their lives if they cannot get the treatment they need. But — here is the mystery — where are the bodies? I mean, of those who died in Opera Square?"

We both stared at him.

"Think," he went on. "Can you have two hundred people wounded and not one killed? I would expect at leasty fifty, perhaps a hundred. And we know, from eyewitness accounts, of known individuals whose friends saw them shot down. Sometimes those friends managed to carry their bodies away. More often they could not."

I remembered the frantic scene with a shudder. It had been every man for himself. I remembered the desolate streets this morning. The dignified old lady trying to construct her own little shrine of flowers and candles in the corner where she had been told her grandson had died. The notices on the unopened shops, where clearly some member of the family had been among the casualties.

"All over the town there is mourning," said Uncle Sandor, "mourning for those who did not come home last night. Some may be in the hospital wards — but families can quickly check that by enquiring. Others — again the sort likely to be on the Securitate files — may have gone into hiding for the time being. Very sensible! But can anyone convince me that there are *no* dead? And, if there are, where are the bodies?"

It was a mystery. But to countless people in Timisoara it was more than a mystery, it was anguish. I learnt in those terrible days that there can be a strange consolation in a dead body. People know the worst and have something to focus their grief upon – a funeral to hold, flowers to bring, an outlet for tears, something to *do*. It is the not knowing that is hell. There was plenty of that in the city.

Nadia asked Uncle Sandor what news there was of the pastor. I felt guilty. I had almost forgotten the man whose persecution had led to this tragedy.

The old musician had not. Nor had the pastor's other loyal supporters. Somehow links had been maintained. The Securitate had men all round the farmhouse to which he had been taken. It was floodlit throughout the hours of darkness. Yet somehow Tokes was getting messages out. The police were still trying to bully him to appear on television, declare he was being well treated, and appeal to the public to give up their protests. His will was unbroken.

"He has a hidden radio," said Uncle Sandor. "He'll be getting these same foreign bulletins – he'll know how the support is building up for him."

I thought of Holy Joe. He would have passed on my unfinished message to his uncle. The Bishop would not dismiss it as some scare story from an excitable school-friend. It would tie up with the first news flashes now reaching the West. My contribution might not add much – a mere pebble thrown into a big pool – but as there were no foreign pressmen in Timisoara any eyewitness account should count for something.

I wondered, should I try to get through to Joe

again? There was much more to tell him now – the shooting in Opera Square, the eviction of the pastor.

I realized sickly that I was being hopelessly optimistic. If I had been cut off yesterday, when not even a shot had yet been fired, what chance had I now to get any such information out? The operators would be more vigilant than ever.

Another thought came and cheered me up considerably. By tomorrow afternoon I should be out of Romania, able to do something really effective, professional almost. I'd call the BBC, I told myself excitedly, ask for the news editor. The words marshalled themselves in my brain. "I left Timisoara – in Romania – only this morning. I thought you might be interested..."

They would be interested all right when they heard the name Timisoara.

It was intoxicating. Bubbling, I confided my plan to Uncle Sandor.

"But how can you be out of Romania tomorrow?" he demanded. "Don't you understand? Our frontiers have been sealed by order of the Comrade. No one comes in – and, I think you will find, nobody goes out."

CHAPTER
SIXTEEN

Uncle Sandor's forebodings were fully justified.

He rang the railway station, then the local airport. There would be no trains, no planes. It was not only in Timisoara that there was a state of emergency.

Nevertheless the Romanian television was trying to keep its own viewers in the dark, pretending that all was normal. The news bulletins, as usual, were full of Ceausescu's doings.

"He has gone to Iran!" cried Nadia incredulously.

"It is apparently a public visit," said Uncle Sandor. "It has been arranged for some time. He's not going to cancel it just because of what's happening here. He adores these foreign trips – they make a fuss of him, he feels like a king."

I was more concerned with my own predicament. Could I at least get a call through to my parents? I was not too upset about being delayed here a little longer. Things were getting rather interesting. And, though I was torn two ways, I was not that keen to leave Nadia. So long as I could let my people know that I was OK and they were not to worry.

I couldn't use Sandor's number for international calls. When we left him Nadia and I parted for a little while – better not to be seen together when I made the call – and I went to a different hotel from the one where I'd been cut off while talking to Holy Joe. Nadia recommended the Continental, in the Boulevard 23rd August – it was big, cosmopolitan and impersonal, so I'd pass unnoticed.

No luck. The people at the desk were evasive. They would not say, in so many words, that outgoing calls to other countries were not being accepted, but they held out no hope of getting me a line in the immediate future.

Being, I suppose, the principal hotel in the city it housed the only Comturist shop. I consoled myself by buying some sweets for Pavel.

I might have been wiser to get cigarettes to improve Josef's temper. He came home from work already badly rattled. The plant was in a ferment after last night. The day's work had been paralysed as rumours ran from department to department. Men were talking the wildest, most dangerous nonsense. Now I told him that my departure tomorrow was delayed.

"Perhaps," he suggested eagerly, "your embassy could help? Surely in these matters strings can be pulled?"

"There must be other stranded British citizens. Maybe a shortage of strings to pull."

"Would it not be easier if you were in Bucharest?"

"The railways are all disrupted, it seems," said Ana, "it might be a terrible journey."

"I'm sorry if I'm being a nuisance," I began.

"You have brought colour into our lives," Ana insisted. "God knows, we can do with it."

Josef tried to assert himself. "I must consider. It may be uncomfortable now for a foreigner in Timisoara."

"It must often be that," said Ana tartly.

"I mean, because of this unrest. We are told it has been stirred up by foreign agitators – "

"We are told a lot of stupid things. Does Greg look like an agitator?"

"I do not say that, Ana. But he was in that demonstration—"

"He was nearly shot, yes. That would have been something to tell his ambassador!"

"You can be a very foolish woman. This is a very awkward time for a man in my position. Things may be worse tomorrow. The hotheads at work are talking of a walk-out in protest..."

I got to my feet and said very quietly, "Perhaps I'd better move to a hotel tomorrow."

I did not want to rush off impetuously to Bucharest, even if there was a train to take me. I should probably only find myself stuck in the capital for days, standing in queues at the embassy, being fobbed off with apologies and

155

excuses. Bucharest without Nadia would be no fun at all.

"Thank you, Greg, but there is no need." Ana glared at her husband. "He has a British passport, yes. And how many of us would envy him! That is the Comrade's great achievement. But before that, Greg is 'family'. He is not only Nadia's cousin, he is mine. I do have some say in who stays under this roof."

There was more resemblance between the sisters than I had previously realized.

"Let us see if there is anything fresh on the news," said Josef hastily. There was not. Because, of course, he was too scared to switch to foreign stations. We should have to go round to Uncle Sandor in the morning to keep abreast of the situation.

We could hear noises from the city centre. No gunfire, but shouting and singing. The population was recovering from the paralysis which had followed yesterday's shooting. By nightfall courage had mounted. Under cover of the dark, the crowds had come back to the city centre, marching up and down, taunting the police and troops. We heard this only the next day. That evening, we stayed in and supported Ana.

We knew how easy it would be for trouble to flare up again at a moment's notice, and for the generals to crack down on it with more shooting and maybe by proclaiming a curfew, ordering everyone indoors. If we were caught on the wrong side of the town it might be impossible to get back at all. It would be unfair to Ana to risk it.

She went to bed fairly early. So did Josef. Nadia and I stayed together for another hour, talking in low voices.

"This is a miserable end to your Romanian visit." Then she corrected herself with a smile. "Well, not *miserable* –"

"No!"

"I wish it had been pleasanter for you."

Pleasant, I thought, was a feeble middle-aged sort of word. "It has been interesting," I assured her. "Interesting – I'll say!"

"A lot has happened in just one week."

"You can say that again!" I thought back to the night of the concert, my close-quarters encounter with the Comrade, my walks with Nadia, the man who had trailed me to my hotel afterwards... There'd been a great round moon over the rooftops of Bucharest and even now it was only getting into its final phase above the citadel of Timisoara...

"You'll have a lot to tell your mother."

"Yes."

I should really enjoy telling Mum lots of things, but I was not sure about all.

We went on for some time longer, talking about this and that. Then we said goodnight and I spread out my makeshift bed on the sofa.

In the morning we started out for Uncle Sandor's early. The troops were still everywhere. Tanks and armoured cars commanded road-junctions, some trundled round the streets on patrol. Uniformed figures stood about, avoiding hostile stares. The old lady had replaced her flowers and candles in Opera Square. We saw similar memorials with women keeping vigil. Friends – or complete strangers – would pause and cross themselves, even place another candle. The embarrassed soldiers pretended not to notice. Even the Securitate did not interfere.

Nadia said, troubled, "I wish we'd rung Uncle Sandor..."

"He won't have gone out yet. He'll be glued to his radio."

"I expect so. All the same..."

"You're not – scared of something?"

"One's never sure, Greg. He's not really a 'political' – but he has friends of the wrong sort, from *their* point of view. And he had that warning, about playing Hungarian music."

I knew that she *was* scared. We quickened our steps, though it seemed wiser to slow down when we saw policemen in front. I was relieved when we reached the tall old house in the side-street and saw nothing unusual. We rang the bell. The dry voice came floating down to enquire our identity. "Come up, my dears, and welcome." The door swung back and we started up the stairs.

As expected, he was monitoring the foreign broadcasts. "It is like an auction," he said grimly. "The numbers go up and up. Twenty thousand deaths – so far!"

I gasped. "Is that possible?"

"Of course not. It is crazy. Guesswork. What

can they do but guess? The newsreaders admit there are no correspondents here because none can get across the border. They are picking up any crumb of rumour that comes to them. From long-distance truck-drivers, smugglers even. Some people will always find a way across frontiers, however tightly they're sealed."

"I wish to God *I* could," said Nadia. "If only I'd got that passport when I applied – "

The sudden violent emphasis in her voice reminded me how strong her feelings were. I hoped she would never be tempted into some hopeless, heroic adventure. I thought of her that night in Opera Square, waving her tattered flag. I went cold. If things had gone differently she could have been tattered herself, flesh shredded by one burst of machine-gun fire.

Meanwhile, whatever sensational reports circulated abroad, here in Romania the news continued bland and reassuring. "Everything is normal," said Sandor with heavy sarcasm. "Disrupted train services, cancelled flights, closed frontiers – who worries? Who goes abroad anyhow, except Party reliables – and the Ceausescu family?"

I had never realized before how numerous that family was. Only Sandor talked frankly about them. And he only dared to, he admitted, because he had a clever young technical friend who periodically went over the flat for him and checked that no one had planted any bugging devices. The Comrade's relatives, in-laws and general hangers-on formed a network with soft jobs and privileges in every sphere of life.

"That is how he buys loyalty," said Sandor. "Why he feels secure enough to go gadding off to Iran."

Even the events at Timisoara had not upset his programme. The Romanian radio announced his arrival at Tehran. Later, on television, we saw him feted as guest of honour by President Rafsanjani, seated on a gilded sofa.

Sandor had no rehearsal that morning, and there was to be no performance at the opera house that evening. Timisoara was a city of mourning.

The missing bodies were still a source of anguish to countless families and their friends. Sandor, his sharp old ear ever close to the ground, was not long in picking up the murmur of a possible explanation. Someone had seen bodies being stacked in an army truck and driven out of the city a few hours after the massacre. His informant could not say how many bodies or in what direction they had been taken.

"It's vague," said Sandor, "and we've no means of checking." If it were true, though, it suggested a smaller number of fatal casualties than we had feared. "Maybe one day we shall know the truth," said Sandor. As it turned out, it was only a week or two before the story was confirmed. The deaths in Timisoara totalled ninety-seven − bad enough, but not the huge massacre we had dreaded.

When Josef came in from work that first day he seemed more uneasy than ever. The atmosphere at the plant had been electric. Things were at a standstill. Nobody wanted to do anything but call meetings and pass votes of protest. "Production figures will be terrible," he wailed to Ana. Production figures dominated his life. The management loved him, but today the workers had jeered him and defied his authority. I felt sorry for Ana. It must be hard having to be loyal to a husband you can't honestly admire.

My presence merely added to Josef's anxiety. After supper I tried to help. "I'll see if I can get through to the embassy," I said. "Perhaps they can advise what I should do."

"A good idea," he said. He did not invite me to use his phone. I could imagine why.

"I'll try the Continental again. If that's no good I'll see if the other hotels..."

Nadia jumped up. "Are you going with him?" Ana asked doubtfully.

"Of course. It sounds quieter tonight."

I said nothing. I would not have pressed her, for Ana's sake, but I was delighted that she was coming.

So along the boulevard we went once more, past the Orthodox Cathedral, its gilt-patterned spires glinting under the moon ... up into the steep-gabled town. I can retrace every step of that walk which was becoming so familiar. Every detail remains in my memory. I imagine it always will.

We swung right for the Continental, which stood east of the other big square with its statues and baroque town hall. This was very much the city centre, with both the other cathedrals and several museums located in the adjoining streets.

There were always crowds in this quarter and tonight they were denser than usual. The men in uniform looked jittery.

There were people standing in the hotel entrance. We had almost to push our way inside. While I tried for my call to Bucharest Nadia dropped back and tried to make herself unobtrusive.

I got through quite quickly. The man at the embassy was polite, even solicitous. Where was I? Timisoara! That got him interested, keener to ask questions than answer them. I got the feeling that they were holed up in Bucharest themselves and did not know as much as they'd have liked about the situation elsewhere. When I mentioned the Youth Orchestra he hurriedly asked my age. There might be trouble for someone if they let anything nasty happen to me.

"Certainly," he said, "we can let your parents know, tell them you're safe and well. Just held up." For the time being, if British citizens were not in danger, they would do best to stay where they were. Once normal conditions returned, I could depend of course on any appropriate assistance to proceed with my journey.

Blah-blah, I thought to myself as I hung up. But what else really could he say? So long as the Comrade had not cut *their* links with England, and they told my family there was no need to worry, that was all I asked.

I glanced round for Nadia. She was not only unobtrusive, she was no longer in sight. But there was a considerable noise going on in the boulevard and everyone was hurrying out of the foyer to discover the reason. I went after them, and, as I expected, caught up with Nadia.

A tank was driving down the middle of the road, surrounded by a laughing crowd. A grinning face protruded from the open turret. Another young man was rather precariously perched behind, waving a flag to and fro with long majestic sweeps. Needless to say, the flag had a hole torn out of the middle.

Nadia explained, delightedly, "They've hijacked it while the crew were having coffee! They're driving round the town!"

A young woman's voice cut in from behind me. "Hi! You speak English?" Brisk, but friendly. And unmistakably British.

"Yes."

"Thank God for that! Can you tell us what the hell's happening here?"

Even at that distance from the lighted entrance I could see she had red hair. She was small and wiry. By contrast the man at her elbow was about the tallest and hunkiest I had ever seen. I had the feeling that they were together. He was concentrating intently on the tank as it passed, and suddenly his two great hands went up in front of his face, though it could hardly have been to shield his eyes. The lights were not that bright.

Nadia was giving the young woman a quick explanation. The stranger was listening avidly. Then she began firing questions. "You live here? But you've been here for the past few days? Fine!

You're a treasure! Do me a favour, ask this old man – "

Nadia became an interpreter. In the next few minutes she questioned three people and translated their replies. Then the young woman said, "Come in, have a cup of coffee! This is too lucky. I'm not losing you. This your boyfriend?" She belatedly remembered my existence.

"My cousin," said Nadia primly.

The redhead plucked the big man's sleeve, looking up as though at some remote crag. "Come back to us, Rolf," she commanded. "We're going inside. Did you get anything?"

A low, amiable voice rumbled down to us, Scandinavian I guessed from the sound of the English. "It'll be out of wack – I had to grab what I could." He was slipping something inside his coat. I saw then why his hands had flown up like that. He held a miniature camera and had to clear the heads in front. His height must be a great asset.

In the bar we all introduced ourselves over the coffee. "I'm Linda," said the woman. "This is Rolf." She did not offer surnames. Nadia asked eagerly, "Are you journalists?" Linda raised a warning finger.

"How could we be?" she said with bland innocence. "Aren't they stopping them all at the frontier?" I had the feeling she would not be an easy person to stop.

We talked with our usual care. Lots of eye contact. The bar would be bugged, but in that babbling crowd it would be hard for anyone to disentangle one thread of conversation. Occasionally Linda scribbled something, mostly she just listened – and prompted. She must have had a wonderfully trained professional memory. She questioned me too. I think she saw a special angle in the concert tour. She wanted my full name, age, home town, the lot. I could see myself providing her with a paragraph or two as an eyewitness of the shooting in Opera Square.

Nadia, though, was her real discovery. Nadia could interpret fluently with any of the locals, as I with my less idiomatic Romanian could not.

"It's a real headache, the language business," said Linda. "I can get by in French and German, but I never know where I'll be sent at a moment's notice. I mean, you can't learn *Romanian* just in case. How do you manage, Rolf?"

The huge shoulders shrugged. "I get by. With my English." He grinned. "And I speak Swedish like a native!"

I gradually pieced out the connection between them. They had run into each other on various occasions, being on the same assignment in this country or that, but they were not working for the same paper. They had met again only yesterday in Belgrade and decided to team up.

"So –" she lowered her voice. "We took a chance, it came off, and somehow – I won't go into details – we've made it as far as here. we've got a hire car, we've got a full tank, and Rolf is a demon driver. So tomorrow, soon as we've made up some sleep..." She paused. "I've a hunch that the big story won't be here. Thanks to you two, I've got what I want on Timisoara. If anything really serious develops it'll be in Bucharest. So at first light tomorrow – before first light, in fact –" She looked very hard at Nadia. "I've got a proposition."

"Yes?" Nadia's breathless answer was almost inaudible.

"If I make it worth your while – and the people I work for will make it *very* worth your while – I must have someone to interpret... Rolf has a road-map, but there could be difficulties on the way..." She glanced at me. "Your cousin could come with us for the ride."

"That would suit me fine," I said. "I'll be better placed for when the frontier opens again." I smiled at Nadia. "I'm sure Josef will be much relieved."

We arranged to be at the Continental at 6 a.m.

CHAPTER SEVENTEEN

Nadia, I am sure, would have gone for nothing — for the sheer adventure. But to be paid for it! By a great western newspaper! That was dazzling. She saw a prospect of innumerable fine-quality tights from Comturist, coffee beans, toilet luxuries and everything normally beyond her reach.

Ana took our announcement with a mixture of regret and relief. She was glad for her sister's sake at this exciting opportunity, only sad at her departure, though Nadia assured her that somehow she'd get back by Christmas, now only six days away. The relief we knew was on her husband's account. Josef was having troubles enough at work without the embarrassment of a foreign guest under his roof.

For this final breakfast we all sat down together. Ana plied us with what food she had — even made us share one of her precious eggs. It would be such a long drive, and in winter...

"You forget," said Josef sourly. "They are with these rich foreign tourists. They will lack for nothing!" Needless to say, he had no idea that our travelling companions were journalists. He'd have denounced them to the Securitate at once.

Ana was worried that I had no scarf against the cold. She offered me one of Josef's, but Nadia stepped in quickly with a plain brown scarf of her own. "It is quite unisex," she assured me, looking up with one of her private grins as she knotted it under my jaw. "There!" I kissed Cousin Ana and Pavel, and we rushed out into the dark.

The blue Mercedes was already at the hotel entrance, Rolf checking everything methodically. Linda's face lit up when she saw us.

"Fine!" she cried.

"You did not doubt us?" said Nadia reproachfully.

Linda shook her head. "Why should I? I'm not often wrong about people." She turned to me. "We'll sit in the back. Your cousin will have to sit with Rolf." Rolf was by now bending over the road-map with Nadia, and their heads were nodding vigorously.

"OK," he said at last, "let's go."

I envied him at the wheel of the Mercedes, but as the long journey unrolled under our wheels, and we met sheet ice and other hazards, besides the sheer mileage and an unfamiliar road, I was thankful enough to be sitting behind this confident, gentle Scandinavian giant.

It was dark for the first couple of hours, with

nothing to see but the white-painted tree-trunks in the headlights, endlessly flickering past. But Linda was an interesting companion. For one who had arrived in Romania at such short notice she had sized up the situation with amazing speed. That day, sitting beside her, I learnt things about Romania I'd never grasped before.

When day broke we got longer views over the forest-clad mountains. At mid-morning we stopped at a village and Nadia managed to raise some coffee. The far-sighted Linda had got the hotel to fill her own flask, but it was better to keep that in reserve. Rolf too needed a break from driving and Nadia took the chance to call Uncle Sandor. She came back with shining face.

"The troops are pulling out of the city!"

Linda stared. "You mean Timi—?" She checked herself, "Where we were last night?"

Nadia nodded. "He says that it was the men at the plant where my brother-in-law works – they threatened to blow up the plant if the soldiers didn't leave the town by eleven."

"This morning?" Linda looked at her watch. "It's that now!"

"They should be gone then. Uncle Sandor says the columns were driving out by first light."

Rolf for once broke his silence. "This plant – what do they do there?"

"It is petrochemical."

Rolf grunted. "Then I am not surprised the army quit. If a plant like that had gone up it would have taken out half the city. What a picture!"

"Ghoul!" said Linda. "But you haven't missed anything. Luckily."

"I am glad," he said meekly. "I do not like disasters. But if they happen I must do my job."

"Me too."

Both our new friends seemed a little shaken by Nadia's news. Linda confessed she had been wrong in assuming that there would be no further developments at Timisoara. The workers' defiance of the army – successful defiance, it appeared – made quite a story. But she decided that on the whole she had probably still been right to make for Bucharest. At least, she consoled herself, she had an exclusive on Timisoara, if only she could get it out before it was picked up abroad. It would have been hard to get it out from Timisoara itself. There'd be more chance of putting her call through from some other town along the road, or at worst from Bucharest when we got there.

Our coffee-stop had not gone unnoticed – or unreported. Ten miles along the road a little black car was drawn up at the verge. A man got out and held up a hand.

"Police?" said Rolf.

"Securitate," said Nadia in a tight little voice. "They always drive about in these Dacias."

"OK." He slowed down obediently. "Linda will do the talking. I am now the stupid Swede."

Afterwards, Linda insisted that Nadia and I had been the talismans that got them through without trouble. "You both give an impression of youthful innocence – however misleading –

and your respectability sort of rubbed off on us. After all, no sensible journalist or foreign agent would hamper himself by going round with a couple like you!"

Nadia *was* naturally invaluable, being Romanian, and with a helpful knowledge of English. But the two Securitate men focused their main interest on me – my British passport, my exit visa all correctly made out. I told them I had already contacted the embassy about my plight and was now trying to get to Bucharest with the help of these kind friends. The policemen wagged their heads approvingly. I was doing the right thing. They didn't want trouble, either for themselves or for me. They didn't challenge Linda and Rolf's claim to be ordinary tourists and congratulated me on falling in with such helpful companions. They even assured Nadia that they would not worry about me now. They became oddly like two benevolent uncles.

The cigarettes merely added a friendly atmosphere. You can't *bribe* the Securitate, of course. But Rolf used the excuse of our stop to light up a king-sized Kent himself, after which it was only good manners to offer them round – and common sense not to notice that the men were filling their pockets from the carton. Then they waved us on with cordiality. Which does not come easy to Securitate types.

We all relaxed a little after this episode. The scenery was rather splendid. The southern Carpathians, snow streaking the skyline heights, the last colours of the autumn still blazing on the lower slopes... This was my country, well, one of my countries. I hadn't felt much pride in it so far, but I looked forward to telling Mum – and other people – about this.

The twilight began to gather. Linda took a turn at the wheel. The rhythm was soothing. I woke with a start, suddenly alarmed. Had we been stopped? But it was only for petrol. When our friends had managed to slip discreetly across the frontier they had bought plenty of coupons at the dollar rate. We were spared the delays that other drivers suffered. We surged on for Bucharest.

How far was it? I could never remember all the places we passed through. It was maybe about six hundred kilometres, surface bad in stretches, hold-ups for this reason or that, a broken-down truck or an endless military convoy. We took a leisurely break in hopes of a decent meal.

"He's back," Nadia whispered when she rejoined us at the table.

"Who?" I asked.

"The Comrade."

"So he's taking it seriously now," said Linda.

Ceausescu's state visit to Iran had only begun on Monday. This was still Wednesday.

"He's coming on television at seven," Nadia warned us.

We ate as fast as the service allowed. It would probably peter out altogether once the Comrade's all-too-familiar face loomed on the screen. We managed to get good seats. Nadia sat between the two journalists to interpret for them. I crouched

172

behind her. What I could not understand straight from the Comrade's own lips I could fill in from her translation.

The President looked haggard, older than when he had walked so importantly along the respectfully lined-up orchestra only a week ago. It could hardly be jet lag, flying from Iran. He must have had a real shock. Had the bloodshed shaken even him? He was supposed to be all for the iron fist. More likely the shock had been the reaction of the petrochemical workers, forcing his troops to pull out so ignominiously.

He was ranting hoarsely, he rambled, lost his way in mid-sentence. The disorder at Timisoara, he thundered – the place was actually being named now – was due to "international terrorist activities", "imperialist reactionary elements menacing socialist Romania". There were "traitors ready to sell our country for a handful of dollars". The soldiers had shown great patience, been "forced to defend themselves". The disgust in Nadia's undertone was eloquent as she translated this flow of verbiage.

It ceased. The face faded, the patriotic music swelled up. Linda turned to Rolf. "What do you think?"

"I'm surprised," said Rolf thoughtfully. "Could it be just strain? If I was covering a boxing match I'd say he was almost on the ropes. I'd be ready for the k.o."

"Unfortunately it isn't a boxing match. There's no one else in the ring."

That was the trouble. There was no one standing

up to the Comrade. It was fine to chant slogans and wave flags, I thought dejectedly, but only Ceausescu had the tanks.

Linda stood up. "Anyhow, my hunch was sound. Bucharest is where we've got to be tonight."

It was a clear run now. Nadia could fold up the map and relax. I saw her head nodding in front of me. Soon I was nodding too, then jerking back to wakefulness, then not even waking. Rolf was driving again. Linda catnapped beside me. Her job had taught her to snatch sleep when she could, but when she did open her eyes she was instantly alert.

Once I woke to find her talking briskly to the back of Rolf's great flaxen head. Which hotel, when we arrived?

"Inter-Continental?" he suggested.

"Too many stairs!"

I thought it an odd, grandmotherly objection. The hotel was one of Bucharest's most modern landmarks, soaring up to over twenty floors. But had she never heard of lifts?

She had certainly heard of the constant power-cuts. "If a story suddenly breaks," she said, "I want to be out and about. I know the press always heads for the Inter-Continental, but – " She hesitated.

"Where then?" he asked good-humouredly.

"I thought the Athénée Palace."

I'd seen that too, across the street from the concert-hall. An old-style classy hotel with balconies, only about six floors but unmistakable.

174

Its name ran along the roof in bold square letters cut out against the sky. It looked over the vast square to what had once been the royal palace.

"I believe it was *the* place in the old days," Rolf admitted, "in King Carol's time. And then in the war it was filled with all the top Nazis. But that's history, the palace itself is a museum."

"I don't care two hoots about the King's palace. I'm interested in another building on that same square – where the Central Committee of the Romanian Communist Party is based."

"Ah!"

"That's the nerve-centre now. The hotel's opposite. If we can get front rooms we'll have ringside seats."

"A photographer's dream!"

"So I thought."

Linda leant forward and woke Nadia. "You said you had your own room in Bucharest?"

"Yes."

"OK. We'll make sure of our hotel first, so you'll know where to find us tomorrow." Our services were already booked. Nadia was essential to interpret street-corner interviews. I too was useful from time to time. "Then Rolf will run you home. And Greg?" Linda forgot nobody.

Nadia and I had already settled this point. At this late hour it might be awkward – or positively unwise – if I turned up at my previous hotel, especially as I was supposed to have left the country several days ago. The porter would immediately get on to the Securitate. Much wiser if, for tonight at least, I went to Nadia's.

It was nearly midnight when we drew up outside the Athénée Palace. Our friends marched purposefully up the steps and through the revolving doors. "This is fun," said Nadia, though we were both yawning our heads off. Soon Rolf was back with a porter trotting at his heels for their bags.

"All OK?" I asked Rolf as we directed him down the Calea Victoriei.

"Fine. Two front rooms facing across to the Party building. One with a balcony – gives me wider angles." He laughed. "Trust Linda. I have found the right colleague." We had realized that. Rolf was a little short of the aggression a press photographer needs. Linda had a genius for fixing things.

Nadia asked him to drop us off at the corner of the Strada Lipscani. It would be best to make our arrival unobtrusive. The Mercedes would not have helped.

"Linda said ten o'clock, if you can make it."

"We will," I promised.

"Good night then. Sleep well."

"Don't worry, we shall," we said together. The car turned and slid silently away. Half staggering over the cobbles with our bags, as though we were drunk and not just dead-tired, we covered the last few yards of the long day's journey.

CHAPTER
EIGHTEEN

Nadia's room was cold and stuffy. The window was sealed with putty for the winter. Though, she declared, there was a joke now going round the city, "don't open the windows or the people in the street will catch cold". December temperatures in Bucharest usually hovered around freezing.

She lit the obsolete little gas fire. Better than nothing. There was no central heating. Luckily we had eaten as well as we could at our wayside stop and Linda had pressed her vacuum flask upon us with enough milky coffee left for a cup each. Nadia tried the tap. At least there was running water. Often the supply was cut off for long spells. She heated enough for us each to have a sketchy wash.

"I could not sleep if I had not at least washed my face," she said, stifling a yawn. I felt that I could, but accepted the offer. She gave me a cushion and one of her blankets and found me another. "I hope you will be all right," she said dubiously.

"I'll be fine," I said. "I've often slept on the floor after a party." I took my torch and found the noisome little cubby-hole under the stairs. When I returned, Nadia had only just begun to undress. I started to back out apologetically, but she hissed, "Don't be silly, shut the door – it is no different from the beach. Perhaps – who knows? – we may be living through a revolutionary situation! There is no time for conventions." She switched off the light and we slipped into our pyjamas by the glow of the gas fire. "It would be nice to leave this on," she said wistfully, "but it is too dangerous."

When she was ready I turned it out and lay down on the floor.

"Good night, Greg," she said softly from the darkness.

"Good night." At least I could thankfully close my eyes and surrender to the long siege of sleep.

But the floor *was* hard, hard as the concrete of the Comrade's apartment-blocks. And the air was cooling by the minute.

I was light-headed with weariness. The white-painted roadside tree-trunks seemed to dance before my eyes. I shifted. Why was the human body ever cursed with a hip-bone?

Nadia's anxious whisper rustled in the silence. "Greg? Can't you get to sleep?"

"I shall," I said, without confidence.

"It is like Siberia." I remembered that she had

sacrificed one of her own blankets. "This is silly," she went on. "We shall freeze to death. We are cousins after all."

"Yes, we're cousins."

"I know you will be good – "

"I'm too exhausted to be anything else."

She laughed. "I too. Then let us be sensible."

"OK. Thanks." I crawled towards her voice.

I met her outstretched hand. Cold as my own. "You have your blankets?"

"You bet."

"Then we shall arrange things." She did so, skilfully, in the pitch blackness. "Dear Greg, you are a very *comfortable* person to be with."

This proved to be inaccurate.

Having pulled the combined bedding over us, we turned away with the utmost decorum, only to realize at once that the human body is not designed for packing economically in pairs on a narrow divan facing away from each other. We could not make the slightest movement without bumping each other. Nadia solved the problem by rolling over and snuggling up against my back. This proved more satisfactory.

Later, when I told Holy Joe the full story, he said, "Well, I'll believe you. Thousands wouldn't." He's a cynical devil, Joe.

"I've told you," I insisted, "We were absolutely dead beat."

It was daylight when I awoke. Nadia stopped shaking me. "Sorry, Greg. It's a quarter past nine. And we promised Linda."

She was dressed. She had made coffee, split

some rolls we had saved from dinner last night, and found a nub of butter in her cupboard.

"Sorry there's no milk."

"Black coffee's just what I need."

We bought hot pasties from the open hatch of a bakery and munched them as we hastened up the Victoriei. One never knew how soon one would eat again. The bakery woman said something about a big rally this morning in Palace Square.

Linda already knew about that when we got up to her room – or more strictly Rolf's room next door, because it was the one with the balcony and made the better observation post. We looked straight across the square to the massive block of the party headquarters, from which Ceausescu would address the crowd.

She drew us out on to the balcony. "Safest place to talk," she murmured. "The whole damn place seems to be bugged – even the loos. So mind what you say, inside. Write it down, even. Only don't leave the paper around."

For generations this hotel had been the recognised centre for plotting and espionage. Now, with the help of modern technical devices – an obsession with the Comrade – the building was fantastically well wired for the collection of intelligence. Besides which, said Linda, every member of the staff reported to the Securitate anything they observed of the slightest possible interest.

Nadia, I thought, looked momentarily depressed. It was not the healthiest place for her. But it was too late now to back out of her arrangement with the journalists.

Linda had managed to get a line to London and file an exclusive story on Timisoara. "It helped," she added, "being able to quote eyewitnesses. Especially an English one!" She was smiling like a contented cat.

I stared. "You *what*? You quoted me? By name?" I was startled yet pleased as well.

"Why not? Papers love names, ages, everything." She saw the alarm in Nadia's face. "Not yours," she said quickly. "Might make trouble for you. But it can't hurt Greg." She turned back to me. "Other news editors will read my story, lift anything they can use themselves. Being the first dispatch from Timisoara. If your father doesn't see it in his own paper some friend will spot it and tell him, because of the name."

I heard this with mixed feelings. How much it would please my family would depend on how the general news from Romania developed.

Down in the square the crowd was getting denser every minute. Every factory, Linda had learnt, would be sending fifty people to swell the "spontaneous" demonstration of loyalty to the Comrade. "They'll be sacked if they don't turn up," said Nadia under her breath. These organized parties were forming up in the front, under the balcony of the Central Committee building. They were holding long red banners which we could not read from behind. Nadia could tell us the sort of slogans they would bear. "ON GUARD!", "PROTECT COMMUNISM!" and "HEROIC COMRADE CEAUSESCU!" She had seen them so often. Once, unwillingly, she had been made to carry one.

"Let's go down and talk to a few people," said Linda, "while we can still move around."

We went out and crossed the square. The factory groups were useless for Linda's purpose. They stood in their massed ranks like sheep in pens. In response to her approaches they looked round anxiously for some activist to give the right answers. Nadia did her best to establish real contact, but she was forced to translate the same clichés time after time.

It was different when we retraced our steps towards the hotel and tried the back of the crowd. Here we found more individuality, even outspoken criticism of the government. These people had come along of their own accord.

They were wary at first, watchful for tape recorders, and when Rolf's camera swung in their direction they turned up their collars or looked away. But once the word got round that the strangers were western journalists many pressed closer, keen to have their say. No doubt there were Securitate agents among them, but we were not challenged.

After a spell we went back in. Rolf had to change to a 500 mm lens for the distance, and load with another roll.

By now the Central Committee were lining their long balcony. Beneath them, facing outwards to the multitude of the Party faithful, stood solid blocks of men in riot gear, the uniformed members of the Securitate. Their colleagues, anonymous in their plain clothes, would be dotted amid the general crowd. We could spot the official TV cameramen in places of vantage.

"Wonder if it's going out live," said Rolf. He stepped back into the room and switched on the set. Sure enough, the image that came up was the scene outside the window.

"What would you expect?" asked Linda. "He's laid it on. Instant propaganda. He can rely on the right response."

"The crowd is well drilled," said Nadia.

It was convenient for us. The television coverage gave us the close-up views of the building across the square, the Comrade in his pot-shaped cap of black astrakhan and the hard-faced Elena at his side, his ministers ranged to left and right, the general commanding his bodyguard . . . When the speech began we could hear it much more clearly from the set in the room. Linda could scribble down some quotes from Nadia's translation.

The Comrade seemed to be holding a script in his hand, notes at least, not orating as Hitler and Mussolini used to do. Perhaps he realized how he'd wandered in his broadcast last night, perhaps Elena had told him to get a grip on himself and do better today. Certainly he was coming over better, though his voice was tired. He was thanking the Bucharest Committee for calling this rally to welcome him back from Iran. Now and then he paused for applause. And sure enough it came, the crowd clapping in measured unison, the way he liked.

The crowd in front, that is, who'd brought

the banners. Not the people behind. Under our windows they seemed to be groaning. It started low, then swelled in volume. Soon it was booing. Then came a chorus of shrill, derisive whistles. The storm centre was in front of the Athénee Palace.

It was getting through to the Comrade, even through the clapping between. He was gesticulating angrily. The television gave us the close-up view. We saw one or two distracted figures rush across the screen. The mike picked up the thin, imperious voice of the unlovable Elena. "Stay calm, please!" Intended only for those flurried people on the balcony, the amplified words rang across the whole square. Indeed, across the whole of Romania.

Someone at the station must have thought quickly and acted boldly. The picture on the screen faded, and the sound with it. We were left with only the noise through the open windows. We had to dash out on our own balcony to see the Comrade, now dwindled to a tiny manikin, impotently waving his arms across that sea of heads and lurching banners. Rolf was madly clicking his camera, then changing his long lens to a wide-angled fish-eye, to get a shot of that human sea washing to and fro below us.

Then the television screen came to life again as suddenly as it had died on us. The Comrade had recovered himself, was declaiming from the paper in his hand, warning us of the perils to the State caused by that infamous disorder at Timisoara. The booing and whistling had not stopped, but the microphones picking them up had been switched off. Viewers would hear only the speaker himself and the fervent applause of the front rows.

"Smart work," Rolf grunted.

For the nation at large a near-disaster had been disguised as a technical hitch. But the people actually in the square could not have been fooled. They must realize now the full strength of the opposition and know as individuals that they were not alone in their hatred of the dictator. With their own eyes they had seen him temporarily unnerved.

We watched them drift away contemptuously without waiting for him to finish his speech. When he did so, only those front ranks stood fast to give him the usual ovation. The pictures on our screen alternated between their rapt upturned faces and the close-up of the triumphant Comrade acknowledging them.

I wondered if he was really as pleased as he looked.

CHAPTER
NINETEEN

"So that's that."

Linda picked up the telephone and asked for Room Service. Lunch for two to be sent up at once to Mr Carlsson's room. She intercepted the look I was exchanging with Nadia.

"Don't worry! Rolf and I are going down. I need to get a general sense of other people's reactions. This is for you two. Better you stay up here. Not so noticeable. Also – " she glanced out over the fast emptying square – "you can watch out for anything fresh happening. If so, nip down, Greg, and find me. Try the bar first, then the dining-room."

"OK." I was glad to be doing something to earn my lunch. Especially when the floor-waiter knocked and wheeled it in. Whatever food shortages the rest of the country was suffering, the Athénée Palace was making a brave effort to keep up its expensive standards.

To get the balcony they needed – especially for Rolf's photography – our friends had been obliged to book themselves top-class double rooms. So Nadia and I sat down to our meal in what, a generation or two earlier, would have seemed the last word in showy magnificence. That was the style of the hotel, all marble and mahogany and crystal chandeliers. Rolf's bathroom had gilded taps and a bath as big as an Egyptian sarcophagus, standing on clawed lion's feet.

The waiter fussed about, flapping table-napkins over our threadbare jeans, adjusting this detail and that, anything to delay departure. He was as curious as hell. If all the staff were hand in glove with the Securitate he would naturally want to pick up any information he could about the English woman and her Swedish companion. When he realized that Nadia was Romanian a certain familiarity crept into his obsequious manner. His hotel training was at war with his instinctive contempt for our shabby appearance. When at last the door closed behind him Nadia's pent-up laughter exploded.

"Never thought of having a room like this," I said. "It's like being on honeymoon."

"*I* should not like my room so thoroughly bugged!"

It was nearly two hours before Linda and Rolf came back. During that time we kept an eye on the square outside but saw no occasion to disturb them. At last Rolf's key turned in the door. Linda swept in. "Right! Now we'll take a turn in the streets and find out what the other half is saying."

She had made good use of her time downstairs, especially while she could drift round freely in the bar. But she knew that the clientele of the Athénée Palace were not exactly typical of Bucharest.

On Nadia's advice we made for the Boulevard Nicolae Balcescu. Everybody seemed to be out that sunny afternoon. The broad pavements had knots of people talking excitedly. It was easy to buttonhole passers-by for interview, or to strike up a conversation with some street-vendor in a kiosk. Nadia's appearance helped. She looked harmless as well as attractive. We others aroused interest as obvious foreigners. People were not so cagey as they had been. They were eager to talk to someone from the free world.

"We are not terrorists," they insisted, "we are not in foreign pay. But the shops are empty, our money buys nothing. We want elections again, free elections. This gang of scoundrels steals our very bread – "

Rolf's voice rumbled quietly. "These folk got a sniff of power this morning. Ceausescu was rattled. They could tell."

That was the feeling all around us. There were no agitators standing up and calling for revolution. No one was starting anything. But everyone was hoping that something *would* happen. Nobody wanted to go home. They all seemed to be taking courage from their very numbers. We had walked down towards University Square, where naturally the students were very much in evidence.

One group began shouting, "Don't leave the

streets!" and it became a rhythmic chant spreading down the boulevard.

"Don't leave the streets!"

They knew that if they split up the power they were beginning to sense would ebb away. There were scores of police around, not interfering yet, just watching. I saw a girl student, slim as Nadia, riding on the shoulders of a man almost as big as Rolf, her denimed legs locked under his bearded chin like a scarf. She was handing down flowers to the policemen and they were accepting them with smiles.

Ordinary policemen, these. Not the Securitate. But there were plenty of them about too, some in uniform, many not.

I got separated for a few minutes from my friends. Suddenly I saw something that stopped me in my tracks. A few yards away, mercifully with his back to me, was my shadow of a week ago, the man who had last seen me getting into a cab for the Gara de Nord.

It would be better, I felt, if he did not see me again just now. I hung back, and did not rejoin the others until they had moved on and he had turned away in another direction. I could see that he was tailing some man who had been particularly outspoken in his complaints against the regime.

I said nothing to Nadia, but as we were close to the underground coffee bar I suggested that it would be a good place to meet students. It was too. They spoke more freely down there than anywhere. They were less camera shy, though admittedly Rolf's first flash bulb nearly caused a panic. After that, they all shoved forward to get into the picture. When they looked too self-conscious Rolf was teaching me how to "stunt up the pic" with some little intervention to draw their eyes.

"You two are a real help," Linda assured us.

It was while we were down there that the trouble started in the square overhead. The first we knew was when a crowd of students came thundering down into the subway.

"They say the tanks are coming!" Nadia cried out.

Wild young men were dashing round the bar, gathering up empty Coke bottles. She stared at them mystified. "Molotov cocktails," Rolf explained.

"Where will they find petrol?"

That, I thought, I could easily guess.

We joined the crowd streaming up the steps. Darkness had fallen above. Several cars had been overturned across the width of the boulevard. One was blazing, and I could hear above the tumult the high-pitched warning of a fire-engine on its way. From other upturned cars students were siphoning petrol to fill their bottles.

We could see the tanks above the swaying heads in front of us. To the previous slogans were now added chants of "Timisoara! Timisoara!" All attempts to hush up that story had now been abandoned. The name of the city had become another rallying cry. A second vehicle was blazing fiercely in the road. In the glare I could see tossing flags with that symbolic hole in the centre.

The firing started. Tear-gas, but not where we were. Bullets from machine-guns and Kalashnikovs. We could see people falling, hear the screams, and then the answering roars of defiance. It was Timisoara again, only worse; and bigger, much bigger. There were helicopters, circling like deafening bats against the night sky, or following the straight lines of the boulevards, raking them with their rocket-fire. Once they passed so close overhead that the hot cartridge-cases came spinning out of their Kalashnikovs and stung my hand.

Linda shouted in my ear, "You'd better get Nadia out of this! I don't want either of you hurt."

"What about yourself?" Nadia retorted.

"I'm press – it goes with the job."

But we stayed together, finding what cover we could as we edged our way northwards up the Nicolae Balcescu. The crowd fought back with stones and Coke bottles, hurling them at the tanks like grenades. You could see them curving through the air, their petrol-soaked rags streaming behind like comet-tails. Then the flash and flare as they hit their targets. We ducked and crouched under the answering volleys of bullets. "Poor Rolf," said Nadia afterwards, "he had so much further to duck!"

One can laugh afterwards. We were lucky, even Rolf. When the tanks rolled forward, the demonstrators retreated into the side-streets, and we went with them. Sheltering in a doorway, we confirmed that so far none of us had a scratch. We talked to others who had paused like us to gather breath in the shadows. It was obvious that the crowd's spirit was unquenched.

It seemed to me pretty hopeless with only stones and petrol-filled bottles against the automatic fire-power of troops and police. "But they say that lots of soldiers are not shooting back," Nadia insisted. "Most of them are conscripts – no older than the students." They were utterly different from the hard-bitten professionals of the Securitate. Ceausescu could never be quite sure of the army. That was why he had built up the Securitate as an élite force he could rely on.

We found ourselves quite near the hotel. "Quick conference," said Linda, "while we can talk without being bugged." We clustered round her in another dark doorway. "I've a feeling this is going to be a long night. We'd better make sure of another meal before all hell breaks loose and maybe the kitchen staff pack up."

"That is sound thinking," said Rolf gravely.

"Question is, our young friends here." She turned to us. "Either you'd better get back to Nadia's place now, before things get any uglier, or if you stay with us—"

"We stay with you." Nadia did not hesitate.

"In that case you must stay with us – literally. I don't know whether I'll even go to bed myself – I don't know about Rolf – but we'll see how things go. Like this morning, we'll make the Athénée Palace our base. There's a second bed in my room, and one for you, Greg, in Rolf's."

"Won't the hotel..." I began feebly.

"Hell, we're paying for double rooms! And this is a time of crisis." She turned back to Nadia. "I'd really appreciate it. You're being a tremendous help."

"Greg too," said Rolf. And I knew he was not just being polite. My scrappy Romanian had come in useful more than once.

Nadia looked at me and I nodded. We did not need any private discussion. We'd stick with these two as long as they wanted us. We'd dropped into this adventure. We wouldn't for the world have chickened out now.

"Come on, then," said Linda.

We found the hotel positively buzzing, the staff obviously rattled. There were people badgering the porter with enquiries for friends who were meeting them but unaccountably had not arrived. There were other people who should not have been there at all, but had taken refuge at the sound of firing and were now making anxious enquiries about cabs or overnight accommodation. Many were swapping sensational rumours and stories of personal escapes.

Linda marched us through their midst towards the bar.

Rolf ordered a double Scotch, Linda a small one. Nadia chose *tuica* and I followed her example. The plum brandy was welcome after the scenes in the boulevard.

A dapper, black-bearded man came sailing towards us, very elegant in dark suit and silk shirt, sallow hands outspread, eyes glittering with delight. "My *dear* Miss Howard!" He actually clicked his heels and bowed from the waist. "I was so hoping to catch you. You are dining here tonight? Dare I hope so? I so enjoyed our conversation here this morning."

"Me too." Linda smiled up at him with a convincing display of enthusiasm. "You explain everything *so* well, Mr Miculescu, I'm *dying* to hear more."

My opinion of her slumped. But, I told myself, trying to be fair, a journalist has to be civil to all sorts. This guy – this creep, I instinctively relabelled him – must be what you'd call a useful contact.

Then my estimate of Linda took another downward swoop. She turned to Nadia and (I felt) quite unnecessarily introduced her, using her full name. This was crazy. So far we'd always been so careful to protect Nadia from publicity. Her lack of a residence permit . . . and here was our hard-headed Linda blurting out, "This is the young lady I told you about." Nadia looked as if she'd have liked to sink through the floor.

This Mr Miculescu, however, seemed singularly uninterested in her. He gave her only a stiff little bow – he was so very elegant himself and under these glittering chandeliers Nadia probably struck him as rather scruffy. At least he asked her no embarrassing questions. He turned back to Linda and repeated

194

his proposition that they should dine together.

To my unspeakable horror and amazement Linda said yes.

"In an hour?" she suggested sweetly.

"I shall count the minutes, dear lady."

I drained my glass of *tuica*. I felt I needed it – but it threw me into an uncontrollable and undignified paroxysm of coughing.

It did not look as if this was going to be my evening.

CHAPTER TWENTY

Upstairs in the corridor Linda paused at her door. "Sorry about that." She mouthed the words, all but soundlessly.

Almost as quietly Rolf murmured, "Shall we see you again tonight?"

She controlled her indignation. "You'd better! If I haven't escaped by ten you find which bar we're in and come and rescue me. Earlier, if anything important crops up." She turned and took Nadia's arm. "Come in and share my nice bathroom. We've plenty of time."

"That would be wonderful!" The door closed behind them. I followed Rolf next door.

"You also a bath?" he said hospitably.

"Please!"

"Be my guest."

I think we were all longing for a bath. I know that there had been moments on the boulevard, amid the flying bullets and explosions, when I

196

had broken out in a sweat of fear. In any case the facilities at Nadia's had been only basic.

I said, awkwardly, "I've nothing to change into – for the dining-room . . ."

"Think nothing of it." He was a comforting man, like a gigantic teddy bear.

"Could you – possibly – lend me a tie?"

He looked down at me with his slow smile. He said, weighing his words, "I imagine it is the only item in my wardrobe that would fit you."

"Thanks a lot!"

The hotel was generous with towels. While Rolf pottered about checking and reloading his camera I enjoyed a luxurious soak in the claw-footed sarcophagus. I felt a lot better afterwards. Rolf took his turn and I could hear him wallowing like a sea lion.

I envied him the clean clothes he had laid out on his bed. Linda had sternly discouraged any idea that Nadia and I might dash down to her place for a few things. "I don't suppose any of us will undress tonight. We're like the fire brigade. You can go down there in the morning if there's a chance. If you wander off tonight you may not get back."

That was possible enough. Trouble might flare up at any moment. Nadia and I accepted that. We thought of ourselves with secret pride as temporary journalists.

By the time Rolf had dressed she was tapping on our door. "Wow!" I said softly as I let her in.

Though Linda had other matters on her mind

she had made time for a hasty look through her own wardrobe. The two of them were much of a size. She had found Nadia a dress that would look better in the dining-room than her jeans. Nadia faced me – diffidently? Or expectantly? "All *right*?" I echoed her murmured enquiry. "*I'll* say. Elegant."

She came in and closed the door behind her. "I am to put both of you in the picture." She mimed at the walls to remind us of electronic eavesdroppers. "Our friend thinks she may be on to something. *Her* friend, just now – " She pointed through the floor. She held out an old envelope on which another hand, presumably Linda's, had scribbled "foreign ministry". Rolf wagged his head, tore the envelope across and took it into the bathroom for reliable disposal. Nadia had a slightly worried expression. "I just wish she hadn't told him my *name*."

I tried to reassure her. "I expect it was just conventional good manners." If the black-bearded guy *was* in some government department Linda would have to behave very correctly. If she was after top-level information she would not be worrying about Nadia's lack of that blessed residence permit.

Considering the crisis atmosphere – and the waiters were as jumpy as cats – we three enjoyed our dinner together. I wondered if it had been like this in the London restaurants when my grandfather dined my future grandmother during the Nazi blitz in World War Two. The bombs must have been more dangerous than the occasional sputter of fire that now reached our ears, but the Londoners had been all in it together, facing a common enemy. In Bucharest tonight who was trusting anyone else?

Curious how many men seemed to have brought in small bags or packages which they put on a vacant chair or even on a table. Didn't they trust the cloakroom attendant? Nadia told me later it was an accepted means of camouflaging a tape recorder to spy on the neighbouring diners. The Securitate did it all the time and the waiters naturally did not dare to check them.

That explained something that had specially puzzled me. We had a distant view of Linda with her Mr Miculescu, who was proving a most attentive host. Once, glancing across, I saw him make an impatient gesture to the waiter, whereupon the man whipped round upon some seemingly harmless solitary individual at an adjacent table, seized his bag and carried it out of the dining-room.

We returned to Rolf's room as soon as we had drunk our coffee, so that we could switch on his own portable radio and tune in to the foreign news bulletins. The story of that morning's rally had been picked up from the start. The subsequent disorders had leaked more gradually. Hungary had the first rumours. Now they were coming through strongly on the American and British services.

At ten o'clock Linda had not reappeared. Obedient to orders, Rolf went down in quest of her. Nadia and I sat exchanging apprehensive glances. If Linda was sometimes reluctant to let us out of her sight we were developing a similar concern for her.

It was half an hour before they returned together, Linda much elated and not solely by champagne. "In the end my friend was *most* helpful. Thanks to his influence I got a line — straight through to Sam." She gave us the thumbs-up sign. "Sam" was her code-name for the news desk at her paper in London.

"An exclusive!" I cried incautiously.

She scowled a warning, but good-humouredly. "Isn't that a word they use in *press* circles?" she enquired innocently.

She could not disguise her triumph. At a moment when there were only a few permanent correspondents in Bucharest, and most of the high-flyers were still beating their wings against closed frontiers, she was not only here on the spot but getting her stories out.

Nadia laughed. "Poor man!" She was thinking of the Romanian and how shamelessly Linda had exploited him for her professional purposes.

"I don't know," said Linda, justifying herself. "I think he enjoyed the evening. All these people are worried sick about their own future. They just don't *know*... If they can build up a useful contact with a foreigner — someone who might help them..." She paused significantly. "One can imagine many situations. You can bet *they* can." She scribbled a line or two in her notebook, ripped out the page, and passed it round us silently.

They are not sure they can rely on the army.

General Milea (Min. of Def.) unwilling to order troops to fire. C. can only trust the Sec.

When we had all read it she nodded to me. I went and flushed the paper away. The inside knowledge that she had just picked up confirmed the impression we had formed on the streets. The serious shooting had come from the special units on which the Comrade's power rested.

We all stayed the night in Rolf's room, fully dressed, dozing fitfully but ready for any emergency, making tea or coffee at intervals. Nothing happened outside and there was no point in leaving the hotel until it did. There was always a nasty possibility that some trigger-happy patrol would blaze away at night-walkers in the streets.

With their experience, Rolf and Linda got more sleep than we did. Rolf especially, as a photographer, was used to what the profession called "graveyard watches" or "all-night doorsteps". A hotel room was luxury by comparison.

When Linda really surfaced, soon after six, we seized the chance to suggest that as the city was now waking up we might pay a hurried visit to Nadia's.

"His blessed shirts," Nadia explained wickedly, though she was as eager for a change as I was.

"As good a time as any," Linda agreed. "Armies attack at dawn. Civil unrest builds up later in the day."

We hurried down through the town. The street-cleaners were out, people trudging to work. Routine can't stop entirely for political drama. Humble folk must carry on as best they can, till they get orders otherwise. Or life becomes impossible.

We reached Nadia's without incident. It was still dark enough for us to need the light, such as it was. My bag was already half packed. I'd only to fold my pyjamas and replace my sponge-bag. Nadia did not take much longer. In our haste and carelessness we had not shut the door behind us when we unlocked it and soon we heard a familiar voice from the passage outside.

"So you're back, Nadia?"

"Looks like it!" Denial was useless.

The door was pushed fully open and for the first time I saw the round, putty-coloured face of the inquisitive neighbour. "So this is . . . ?"

"My cousin," snapped Nadia. "From England."

The eyes, black as currants, widened. "This is Mr – Byrne?"

It was Nadia's turn to stare. "How did you know that?"

I could guess. I was flaming angry. I entered into the conversation. "You know because, when I came here before, I was followed back to my hotel afterwards. That man got my name from the register. And, as it was you who'd put him on my tail, he told you as a matter of interest – "

Now Nadia too saw daylight. "I remember now! *Your* cousin, Petre Trofin – who works for the Securitate. He would!"

The woman began to bluster. "I'm sure I don't know—"

"You're certainly not going to know any more. Get out of my room." Nadia pushed her out, with some words that up to that moment I had not known in Romanian. She took a last look round the room, switched off the light, and turned the key behind us. "I never want to come back here," she murmured to me grimly.

Instead of turning left, back to the Victoriei, we swung right to the Nicolae Balcescu. The old instinct – if you think someone may be watching, trick them by heading off in the wrong direction. It was very little further. The two long thoroughfares were roughly parallel. Eventually we could cut through a side-street and come out in Palace Square opposite our hotel.

By taking the route up the boulevard, however, where all the excitement had been yesterday, we saw more clearly the extent to which the spirit of revolt was still alive. There were not many uniforms in sight. The ordinary troops were gone. "Withdrawn to barracks," an old street-vendor assured us. The regular police, the militiamen, were carrying out their normal duties, and the blue cap-bands of the Securitate were nowhere to be seen. As for their plain-clothes colleagues, who could say where *they* were?

"Gone to their rat holes," said Nadia. "They won't be far away."

They had their secret quarters, people said, in different buildings all round Palace Square, with arms dumps, food stocks for a siege, and communicating passages underground. It sounded fantastic. But why should it not be true?

"The Comrade has apartments in the Central Committee building. When he chooses to sleep there he likes to feel safe."

This morning, as the winter sunrise broke over the boulevard, the avenue seemed in the undisputed possession of the people. Already crowds were marching up and down. They were carrying tattered tricolours, chanting the slogans of yesterday afternoon. And roaring that thunderous football-supporters' chorus which was now spreading through Eastern Europe like some modern Marseillaise. There must have been thousands on the streets already.

As we got some distance up the boulevard we saw Rolf unobtrusively taking pictures. He turned back with us towards the Athénée Palace.

"Where's Linda?" I asked.

"Calling her paper again – while she can! Who knows what will happen this morning?"

We made as hearty a breakfast as we could. Our walk in the fresh morning air had sharpened our appetites. We found that we could get an omelette as well as our usual rolls and butter. Linda insisted that we keep Rolf's radio on, turned low, and as we finished eating came the announcement that I think she was expecting.

The government had proclaimed a state of emergency throughout the country.

"So much for the loyal rally yesterday," said Linda quietly. "It was a flop. They can't hide the fact any longer."

And last evening's attempt to intimidate the demonstrators with tanks had been an equal failure. This morning, as we had just seen, the crowds held the boulevard unchallenged. "Throughout the country," Rolf repeated thoughtfully.

"It is an admission that it is not only in Bucharest that things are stirring."

"We must get out and about," said Linda. "If we're challenged we'd better come clean and wave our press cards at them. No use getting ourselves shot."

"Sure. We're here now and they can hardly push us out."

Linda gave us a keen look. "If you two are coming round with us – "

Nadia said, "We are."

"Then you must do exactly what we tell you. No question. You're not covered. You'll be a great responsibility."

"But we may be a great help," said Nadia sweetly.

The radio began another important announcement. We all froze. Nadia let out an exclamation, then translated in a horrified tone. The Minister of National Defence, General Vasili Milea, had been unmasked as a traitor and had committed suicide.

I remembered the scrap of paper Linda had silently passed round last night. It was the man, she had been told, who was reluctant to give the order to fire on the crowd. Only later – this was always happening – did we learn the truth. Milea had not committed suicide. On Ceausescu's orders he had been seized by men of the dictator's bodyguard, dragged to an upstairs room, and shot.

Rolf had stepped out on to the balcony. He called in to us. "Look at the crowd down there!"

The square was a stormy sea of vehement faces

and waving arms. There was none of the regimentation of yesterday's demonstration. No long red banners with their white-lettered slogans. A cordon of soldiers lined the clear space at the base of the headquarters building and for the present the excited crowd was not pressing against them. But, if the troops were put to the test, would they open fire?

"He's coming out!" Rolf shouted. His camera was clicking.

I saw the dictator on the balcony. Same shaggy cap of black astrakhan. He was clutching a loud hailer. He raised it to his lips. The harsh voice boomed out over the square, distorted, to me at least quite incomprehensible. It had been so different that other time, coming to us through the television set.

"We must get closer," said Linda. We streamed out to the lift.

As we reached the square Rolf swore quietly. "I'm going to need more film. Greg, would you mind? I left a fresh roll on my table."

He tossed me the keys as he rushed after the others.

I had a last glimpse of Ceausescu ducking under the hail of missiles. His bodyguard was hustling him to safety indoors. I ran across the foyer, eager to catch up with my friends, and flung myself into an empty lift. My hand went up to the button, the old-fashioned doors began to close, hesitated momentarily as another passenger forced his way in after me, then clanged shut. The lift started to rise.

Then, with no word of explanation or apology, the stranger behind me thrust out his arm to the button. The lift stopped abruptly and began to descend again.

"Hi!" I protested angrily and swung round.

His gun was pointing at me. My fellow passenger was my one-time shadow, Comrade Trofin.

"I did right to try this place first," he said with a self-satisfied chuckle.

CHAPTER
TWENTY-ONE

He had spoken in Romanian. I instinctively
answered in that language. After which, it was
too late to pretend I did not understand him.

"What is this all about?" I demanded.

We had shot past the ground floor and stopped
in the basement. Still keeping me covered, he
opened the gates and motioned me to step out.
"You're under arrest," he said curtly.

One of the hotel staff, a cellar man or something, was coming towards us. When he heard
those words he backed away. He did not want
to know. It was no good my calling for help. No
one would lift a finger on my side.

"I hold a British passport," I said.

He was not impressed. He answered, rather
nastily, "We know that foreign agents are at the
bottom of this." He waved me forward along a
brick-arched passage between racks full of wine.
At a sort of fire door he fumbled with keys, still

holding the gun pressed close against me, and opened the door, locking it behind us as we advanced further into this subterranean world.

"There will be trouble for you," I warned him. "There is nothing against me – I was with the youth orchestra – "

"You have behaved very suspiciously since. You established links with a Romanian subject – which she never reported to the authorities. You pretended you were leaving Romania, but you disappeared without a trace, and now I find you still here in Bucharest. And in a hotel where you are not registered. Linked up with two western journalists – whose entry is illegal, or at least irregular."

Listed like that, it seemed quite a damning indictment.

Over my shoulder I asked, "Why have you brought me down here?"

"For interrogation."

"Down *here*?"

"No." He laughed. "To save you the embarrassment of being marched across the square in view of that scum out there. These passages link all the buildings."

I tried to sound cooler than I felt. "You mean to stop the people lynching *you* and rescuing *me*?"

"You will see, Mr Byrne."

They were fantastic, those subterranean passages, forking left and right or curving on ahead. It was a maze, designed and equipped to stand a siege, with tanks of water and vast food-freezers and steel fire doors at intervals. Rungs set in the concrete walls rose to blank ceilings overhead, but adjacent tool kits and pneumatic drills indicated concealed emergency escape routes in case the inmates found themselves trapped.

It was a weird honeycomb, a secret defensive infrastructure the Comrade had ordered to connect his party headquarters with the one-time royal palace, the university library, and every other large building facing on to the square, even our own hotel. I never knew which of these buildings Trofin was heading for, because we never got there.

Suddenly there was an almighty racket some-where overhead, thunderous crashes, echoing shouts, feet racing to meet us. Three figures loomed, paused breathlessly, greeted Trofin. I caught the phrase, "emergency stations". Trofin stammered a question in alarm. One of them answered, "But they're breaking in!"

Trofin gasped incredulously. Another man explained bitterly. "The Army's let us down. The troops aren't defending the place – they've got orders to pull out –"

"Surely – the Comrade?"

"They're getting him away off the roof – by helicopter. Now it's *our* job..."

My captor's concentration shifted momentarily to these compelling new demands. I thought I saw my chance. There was a terrific crash above us as some heavy door yielded to assault. The chorus of voices was suddenly clearer.

Death to Ceausescu!

The revolver was no longer pressed hard against

my ribs. It seemed a good moment to go. I went —
in what I hoped was the right direction. Trofin
yelled, then fired. The shots made an unholy noise,
reverberating down that narrow subway. I turned
up some steps which I saw, too late, were barred
halfway up by a steel door. Thank God it was
not locked. I pushed through and panted up the
steps towards the yells that now were deafening.
I was not aware of any pursuit. Trofin and his
comrades had lost any zest for it.

I came up into the daylight to find myself in the
vast entrance lobby of some public building, with
an impressive marble staircase sweeping up to the
floor above. There were three tall doors facing the
square. One was broken back on its hinges and
young men were streaming in. Soldiers ran to meet
them — but with upstretched empty hands. "You
want arms? Here you are." The demonstrators
seized on the discarded rifles gleefully.

One man carried a flag with a hole in it. Another
I recognized as Adrian Donea, Nadia's favourite
cab-driver. He seemed to be leading them, and, as
they raced after him up the stairs, I followed.

At the top we came to another grand lobby, with
corridors opening off to right and left. Some shots
rang out. There seemed to be more resistance up
here. Perhaps Securitate, not the conscript soldiers
who had welcomed us so enthusiastically down
below. Some of the demonstrators turned aside,
blazing away with their newly acquired weapons.
Donea and others went dashing straight across to
the open door that faced us, and I went after
them.

We were – quite obviously – in the dictator's office, for there were glass doors opening on to the balcony, and the whole world beyond was a maelstrom of shouting and song. Donea and several others ran out, waving madly. His voice pealed out in some triumphant announcement. The roar that came back was something I shall never forget.

I hung back in the office. It was their great moment, not mine. I looked around me. There was a rich carpet, with a circular pattern, very mud-trodden now and soon much littered as people snatched up official papers, glanced at them, and threw them down. There was a big historical painting of the sixteenth-century national hero, Michael the Brave, on a white horse. There was the Comrade's huge desk in one corner, his very typewriter.

It was an oddly assorted little crowd, that first bunch of people who had found their way into his office. There was a blonde hostess from the Inter-Continental. Others included a sculptor and a portrait painter, an almost illiterate soldier and a sociologist. I learnt all that later because, within a couple of minutes, Linda was there interviewing them.

Nadia looked across at me, both incredulous and relieved. "How on earth – "

"Long story. Tell you later," I said airily.

I must not interrupt her translating, though some of these intellectual types could talk direct to Linda – and volubly.

I had seen Rolf walk through some inner door so

I followed him. He brushed aside my apologies for not having brought the extra film. He had enough for this job. Just look!

It did not at first sight seem to me particularly photogenic. This inner room looked something like a telephone exchange and it was quite true, a few clear shots would be ample to cover the subject.

"But *what* a subject! Wow!" His Scandinavian stolidity for once deserted him. "Do you realize what this room was? It was where he could check up on anyone – anyone – whose phone was being tapped. Even his most trusted lieutenant. If he *did* trust anyone."

"I must tell Linda."

"Sure." With their different lines there was no competition between them.

Before I could break in upon Linda's interview something else did. A man rushed into the office. "The helicopter is still on the roof! He may be still in the building!"

Everyone rushed out into the lobby. I went back to tell Rolf. He must not miss anything.

Someone tried the lift. It did not respond. "Quiet!" he ordered, tilting his head with an intent expression. Down the shaft came frenzied bangings, hysterical voices.

"It's jammed – the power's off."

"Perhaps he's trapped inside it!"

"If we're quick we can still..."

We streamed up the stairs like ravening bloodhounds. I went with the rest. I'd no weapon, but I succumbed to the general hysteria. Our one thought was to catch the monster. Ceausescu should not escape.

As I staggered up the last flight of stairs, I heard an excited outcry from the jammed lift, only feet away from us behind the casing, only feet below the top of its shaft. The helicopter crew had broken open the gates, they were pulling the passengers up and out to freedom.

We reached the windy sunshine of the rooftop. Several helicopters stood ready for take-off, their rotor blades turning. I saw Ceausescu in his blue overcoat, an insignificant figure, his astrakhan cap slanted askew by the struggle, being dragged across the roof. Elena was in front, she was hauled aboard as ignominiously as a sack of flour. Her husband was hoisted in after her. The helicopter took off. The others followed, lurching away into the sky like great bumbling insects, flying off in different directions.

There were five of them. Except for the unforeseen jamming of the lift nothing had been left to chance. No one could guess where the Ceausescus were heading for.

Far below in the square the vast crowd was singing its own words to the Solidarity tune.

Olé, olé, olé, olé!
Where's Ceausescu? Gone away?
Olé, olé, olé, olé!
Yes, Ceausescu's gone, hurray!

I looked at my watch. It was still only ten past twelve.

CHAPTER TWENTY-TWO

Where *had* the Comrade gone?

For the moment, no one knew. Who cared anyhow? He had fled in panic, a broken man. The Army had come over to the people. Everyone was crying out the joyous news.

For the next few hours Bucharest gave itself up to delirious celebration. Open trucks were commandeered, packed with hysterical flag-wavers, and driven madly up and down the boulevards. For the second time in our lives Nadia and I found ourselves dancing together, laughing delightedly in each other's faces, but this time with thousands of other people in the pale afternoon sunlight in Palace Square. Church bells were ringing. An old woman beamed at me, transfigured. "We have not heard that sound for years!"

I caught Linda's eye too. She was thoughtful, almost grim. When we paused for breath beside her I teased her for looking so serious.

"It isn't so simple," she said. "When you've seen as many revolutions as I have, you'll know it isn't all waving banners."

"I know, but – " I was vexed at her pessimism.

"It was all too easy. I don't think that monster is finished. Suppose he hits back?" She could see that I had no ready answer. She pressed on. "Who's in charge now? Somebody has to *run* the country. This is too much like a comic opera."

"The Army's come over, surely? These generals who've been trooping in and out – "

We had stood for a time, watching them as they hurried into the captured Party headquarters. Nadia had done her best, asking round the bystanders, to get Linda the names and ranks of anyone who looked newsworthy.

"They look much the same old gang, who've just quit a lost cause," said Linda. She made an effort to be fair, not wishing to be too much of a wet blanket on the celebrations. Who else, after all, had any experience of running the country? In other East European states where Communist governments were tottering, new popular leaders were becoming known. Who in Romania, for twenty years past, had had a chance to have any public career if they had not been among Ceausescu's yes-men?

"I'm afraid, so long as that man's at liberty," Linda went on, but broke off as the crowd suddenly fell silent and fixed its gaze on the long balcony. Adrian Donea had appeared, holding up a paper, his other hand raised for attention.

"I have a telex, just received, to read to you. It says, *The Comrade and Comradess have been arrested at Tirgoviste.*" A roar of acclamation went up. He grinned down at us, waving the paper. "So your good friend Nicolae Ceausescu may even now be on his way back to Bucharest!" The howl that greeted this was blood-curdling.

So this is it, really, I thought exultantly. It removed the shadow in the background, the haunting fear that somehow the Comrade would still rally his supporters and sweep back to take a fearful revenge.

Linda was asking, where is this place Tirgoviste? Nadia said, "Not so very far – "

Linda looked at Rolf. "What do you think?"

He shook his head. "We'd probably miss him. They'll bring him back here – unless they're afraid of a rescue attempt. If they're afraid of that they won't keep him in Tirgoviste either. They'll move them to a safe place and we shan't know where."

"You think someone *might* try to rescue—" Before she could finish her question she got an answer. Rifles cracked. No one at first could see where the shots came from. People began to run in panic. I was close at Nadia's heels when she went over, sprawled in front of me, and lay still. I dropped to my knees. "Nadia! Are you all right?"

For a few moments there was no answer. But only because the fall had knocked all the breath out of her. Then, "Yes! But, Greg – are *you*?"

Someone cried that men were shooting down from the rooftops. I heard the hated word,

"Securitate!" We scrambled to our feet and ran.

Those shots brought an abrupt end to our rejoicings. They started a nightmare that lasted through the next forty-eight hours.

The Securitate, and only the Securitate, had remained loyal to the Comrade. They had not only gone literally underground but had taken to the housetops as well. After that chase through the subways I understood how their snipers could cease firing from one building and, after a few minutes, open up again from another across the square. The roof was a favourite vantage point but the marksmen might use any upstairs window. There were snipers flitting about in several parts of the art museum. One apartment-block was a positive wasps' nest of the Securitate, for it housed the normal living quarters of many top-ranking members. Once we came back to the hotel to find some of them raking the square from the floor immediately above our own.

They moved about with an impudent self-confidence. Those who normally wore uniform got rid of it. They carried their little automatic rifles neatly folded inside their harmless-looking holdalls. They ranged almost at will through the subterranean tunnel-system, which no one else had time to master while this undercover warfare raged. In arms, training and equipment they were of course vastly superior to the conscripted peasant boys of the regular forces.

I could read the fear in people's eyes as the weekend passed and there was no hard news of the Ceauseascus. What if they *had* somehow got away and were even now welding together these élite troops of the Securitate to establish their power again?

It was not just a local situation, not just confined to Palace Square or even to Bucharest. Nadia called her sister twice that weekend. The first time, she heard that the Securitate men guarding the pastor had vanished from their posts. The second time, that they were sniping at people from their hide-outs in Timisoara. There were outbreaks like that in half a dozen towns. In Bucharest, in those days, the Securitate killed over five hundred people and wounded another thousand. They meant to show us that they were still a force to be reckoned with.

Yet, amid all these alarms, the general mood of celebration reasserted itself in the city. It was, after all, Christmas – and Romanians had never forgotten Christmas, even in the forty-two years in which the festival had been virtually banned. There might be tanks in the streets and no goods in the shops, but it was Christmas. People managed what they could. On Sunday, which was Christmas Eve, they were handing round the traditional thin pastries called *turte*, symbolizing the swaddling clothes in which the Christ child had been wrapped. The television announcer departed from his script to draw attention to studio decorations that had not been seen on the screen for some time, and to the delight of viewers the camera went ranging away to reveal a hastily mustered display such as the children had never seen in their lives.

Over that hectic weekend we seemed to spend a lot of our time down at the television centre. It had become the rival centre for the exchange of news and rumours, the natural rendezvous for all the foreign pressmen who were now allowed across the frontier and were making a beeline for Bucharest. Linda and Rolf were no longer alone. Dozens of their colleagues were competing desperately with them to obtain an exclusive. Desperate and dangerous it was too. There were five journalists among the victims of the Securitate bullets. The television station was no healthier than Palace Square. One wing of it was being used by the temporary new government, so it was an obvious target.

These nightmare conditions lasted till Christmas Day. That evening came – this sounds rather horrible, but it was the grim truth – a news bulletin which was to most Romanians the best Christmas present they could have had.

The Ceausescus had been tried that day and found guilty of a long list of crimes against the Romanian people, including, on their orders, the murder of thousands. They had been sentenced to death and only an hour or two ago they had faced an army firing squad at Tirgoviste.

Now one could really breathe freely. There would be no chance for the Securitate to stage a counter-revolution and bring them back to power.

It was a gruesome end to the story, but I can't pretend that I didn't share in the general feeling of immense relief. Nadia and I, however, had an extra personal reason to rejoice.

Linda came in with her enigmatic smile. "Oh, Nadia – a little Christmas gift – sorry it's a bit late, but I've only just got hold of it."

She held out a flat object which proved, when the fold of gift-wrapping was removed, to be just a stiff, thick manilla envelope. In a dazed, incredulous voice Nadia stammered as she drew out its contents – she could not believe her eyes.

"Just a little spin-off from that working dinner with the elegant Mr Miculescu from the foreign ministry! You really ought to thank *him*. I asked him to look into the unaccountable delay to your passport application – and he was so anxious to oblige that he promised he'd see if he could shift the log jam. He must have done."

Nadia opened the precious document, checked her name as correct, exclaimed at the outdated photograph she had submitted all that time ago.

"I had given up hope! And, look, there is even an exit visa!"

"The most valuable part of a passport in some countries," said Rolf drily.

Nadia's face underwent a sudden change. She looked round at us all. "I don't know what to say – I don't know what to do. Now that everything is changed. Can I leave the country, now that we have achieved this wonderful freedom? Would it be unpatriotic to desert my country? Oh, this is *terrible*! I am torn all ways –"

Linda's eyes were sympathetic, but her voice was as dry as Rolf's. "When you've been a journalist as long as I have," she said, "there's only one thing about the future you're certain about – you're never sure *what* it will bring. Why not take a chance to have a peep at the world outside? You'll be free to come back here when you want – *if* you want."

"Let's talk about it," I murmured. So we went off, the two of us, and did just that.

Telephone communications were getting back to normal. I had already called my parents at Mayrhofen, to wish them a happy Christmas, assure them I was all right and looking forward to celebrating New Year with them at home. We agreed that in present conditions there would be no sense in my trying to join them in Austria – I might not make it in time.

After my talk with Linda I rang them again.

"There's just one thing, Mum," I said as casually as I could. "In the midst of all this hassle I've met up with some of your relatives – in fact they've been very kind and hospitable –" I thought of Josef, but he wasn't really "family". I wanted to get my mother in a responsive mood and of course I did. "One of my cousins wants to grab this chance to get out and see England."

"How sensible!"

"So I wondered, would it be a lot of trouble . . .?"

"Of course not! You know what your father always says, our house is Liberty Hall. A cousin – how exciting! How old is he?"

"My age. Only – he's a she."

"No difference!" said Mum heartily but not, I felt, quite accurately. "Just as welcome."

Nadia was standing so close she heard it all.

Her arm tightened round my waist. I only had to explain the phrase "Liberty Hall" which was unfamiliar to her.

"It sounds a lovely phrase," she said.